L<small>AND OF THE</small> L<small>OST</small> M<small>AMMOTHS</small>

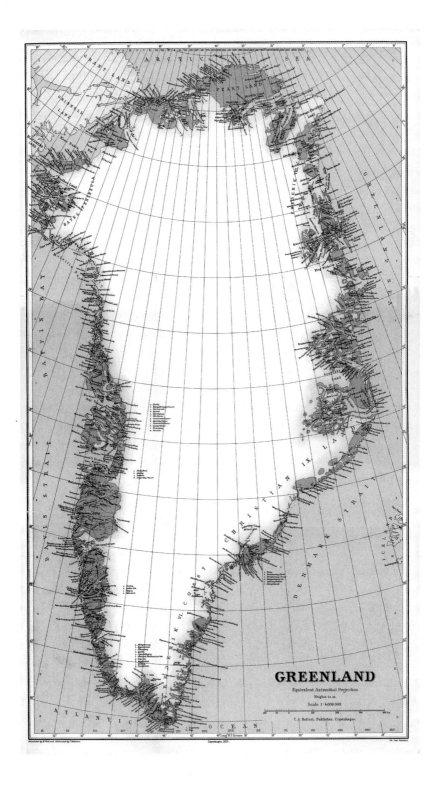

GREENLAND

Equivalent Azimuthal Projection

Heights in m.

Scale 1 : 9 000 000

C. A. Reitzel, Publisher, Copenhagen.

coda

*It was the belief of the East Greenlanders that they themselves
were not the only inhabitants of their land. In fact they believed
themselves to be surrounded by a host of mysterious beings . . .*
KNUD RASMUSSEN (1933)

*The object of the expedition . . . was to explore the East Coast of
Greenland . . . inhabited, by old, of a flourishing colony of Icelanders,
of whom some traces, it was supposed, might still be discoverable . . .*
CAPTAIN WILHELM GRAAH (1837)

*. . . the dwarf mammoths of Wrangel Island raise a new and
unexpected question: could the traditions and the "mammoth myths"
among the indigenous peoples of northern Siberia or Alaska have
come from actual encounters with living animals?*
CLAUDINE COHEN (1994)

)(O)(O)(

LAND OF THE LOST MAMMOTHS

⇒ A SCIENCE ADVENTURE ⇐

MIKE DAVIS

ILLUSTRATIONS BY
WILLIAM SIMPSON

ᴘ ERCEVAL PRESS

LAND OF THE LOST MAMMOTHS

ISBN 0-9747078-0-5
© 2003 Perceval Press
© 2003 Text Mike Davis
© 2003 Illustrations William Simpson

First Edition

Published by Perceval Press
1223 Wilshire Boulevard, Suite F
Santa Monica, California 90403
www.percevalpress.com

Editors: Pilar Perez and Viggo Mortensen
Design: Michele Perez
Copy Editor: Sherri Schottlaender

Printed in Spain at Jomagar, S/A

CONTENTS

*T*his little novel is a bedtime story run amok. It began one magical summer night in Tasiilaq when all the sled dogs were howling, and Jack said, "Tell me a story . . ."

Greenland is beautiful, vulnerable, and infinitely mysterious. It is also the home of some of the most heroic and kindhearted people on earth. They gave Jack and me a vision of hope that we will always cherish.

The story, as it has unfolded, involved some fascinating research, and I break with fiction convention by including footnotes to guide readers curious to know more about trikes, mammoth cloning, lost Vikings, Knud Rasmussen, the culture of East Greenland, Norse magic, ice caves, and more. Within the fantasy there are numerous islands of historical fact and science.

Jack, his brother "Conor," and Julia Monk are real kids—not smarty-pants geniuses like their characters in the story, but action heroes nonetheless. Jack does dream of Greenland, "Conor" does know all about mammoths, and Julia is truly brave enough to face down a sorcerer named Halldor.

Finally, I must warn the reader: Puisortoq, that place of ultimate icy terror, does exist. Remember, it is bad luck even to pronounce the name. And never, under any circumstance, attempt to approach it from the sea.

Unless, of course, you believe in certain odd legends still told by hunters in southeastern Greenland . . .

EPISODE ONE: *The Science Project*

*J*ack was alone on Greenland's Inland Ice. Behind him, the white immensity sloped upward toward the buttermilk Arctic sky. In front of him, however, the glacier abruptly stopped at the edge of a great crevasse, then cascaded downward in giant jagged steps to an ice-flecked sea.

This enormous icefall was an impassable obstacle. Even with ropes and climbing gear, it would take at least three days to descend. Its base, moreover, was simply a birthing platform. Crack! Echoes ricocheted through the labyrinth of crevasses. Mother ice sheet had just given birth to another baby iceberg. Hundreds had been born in the last few weeks, all headed south toward Cape Farewell and the shipping lanes of the North Atlantic.

No, the way ahead was impossible. Jack had no plans to hitchhike on an iceberg back to Dublin. But what were his options? Looking to his left, the ice plateau continued to the horizon. The low Arctic sun outlined countless fissures and cracks. More crevasses, Jack thought. That way is no good either.

To his right, however, the white-blue ice eventually collided with a ridge of black rocks, a half-buried mountain spine perhaps three or four miles away. No crevasses were visible. "Got to hurry," he said to himself.

An hour and half later, he was scaling the icy flank of the rock ridge. What would be on the other side? Another glacier? Or a sheer wall, hurtling down thousands of feet toward a fjord below?

While he had no idea what to expect, with a firm handhold he boosted himself to the top. It was difficult at first to fully comprehend the landscape before him. Nothing in his experience or reading could have prepared him for such a possibility. No fantasy would have been so unreal.

The ridge sloped steeply downward on its opposite side, perhaps two or three hundred feet, into a great glacier-carved trough. It was a hanging valley ending abruptly, to his left, as a high cliff above the sea. Straight ahead and to his right, however, the valley continued for miles before splitting into sloping tributaries that then carried on toward the southern horizon.

The mountains and rocky moraines that ringed the valley all had diamond-shaped patches of snow and ice, but the valley itself was clear, with scores of ponds and a few larger, deep lakes. A necklace of streams at the top of the valley converged into a single current that flowed powerfully for a mile or two until it fell off the ocean edge as a giant waterfall. But this was not the remarkable part.

The valley was also green, amazingly green. Jack could see that it was covered not just with the usual sedge and wiregrass, but with thick heath, dwarf willows, and huge patches of crowberry. More moor than tundra, it was a true Arctic oasis. Yet this was still not the incredible part.

What was truly extraordinary—what challenged the imagination—was the herd of animals immediately below him, perhaps a quarter mile away. Absorbed in the hard work of browsing the dwarf willow and heath, they were oblivious to him watching from above.

They were a family group of five: mom, dad, and three youngsters. The hair of the younger animals was almost as red as that of Jack's cousin, Liam. The parents' hair was a mature gray-black.

Jack had to check himself. He was really seeing this. They were not a hallucination. They were real. And they were mammoths.

2. LATE FOR SCHOOL

Ring! Ring!

"Hey, Jack, time for school!"

"Breakfast!"

His alarm, Mom, and his brother Conor all seemed to be going off simultaneously. He wasn't in Greenland, just snug in his bed in Dublin, Ireland. Yet the image of the mammoth family—as crisp as a photo-graph—lingered for a few seconds in his mind. So real.

"Hey, Mom, I just had an incredible dream."

"Greenland again, Jack?"

"Well, yeah."

Jack's dad—an Irish-American writer who lived in California—had taken him on an amazing vacation to East Greenland when he was seven. It was just the right age to become enchanted by that magic land.

They had climbed mountains, chased icebergs along the shore, and met polar bear hunters returning from places still marked "unexplored" on official maps. Once, while hiking, they had come across a man singing to a dead whale. Several times they discovered stone circles that were the ancient footprints of houses from an Arctic dreamtime before Europeans when Greenlanders thought that they lived alone on an ice planet.

Jack also had watched, a little enviously, as Inuit kids played soccer under the midnight sun while their sled dogs touched noses and wrestled for dead fish. Almost always there was a small red boat in the fjord. It nested in the same spot, under the shadow of a magnificent mountain that looked like the Matterhorn. Night in early August was only two hours long, but full of meteors.

That was nine years ago, but Jack was still haunted by the indelible memories of that summer. Periodically images of Greenland would erupt in his mind. They would cast a spell over his sleep and for a week or two he would dream of nothing else.

"Were you chased by a polar bear again? Or did you fly a helicopter?"

"No, Mom, this was best dream yet. I saw mammoths."

"What species?" Conor yelled from the bathroom. For once, Jack's obsession with Greenland coincided perfectly with his thirteen-year-old half brother's formidable knowledge of Proboscidea, living and extinct.

"I'm not sure."

"Oh come on," said Conor. "Were they pygmies or full-sized? *Mastodon turincensis* or *Elephas premigenius?* The *Mammathus* branch or the *Loxodonta* lineage? Did you notice any molting? How about the curvature of the tusks?"

"Conor, hurry up in the bathroom," Mom interrupted.

"I think they were pygmy mammoths." Jack was trying hard to keep his fast-fading dream in focus.

"I think they were imaginary," said Mom. "Now hurry, both of you. You have to leave for school in ten minutes."

Jack's first class had one student, and he was it.

In the last two years, he had breezed through James Connolly Secondary's entire science curriculum, exhausting the knowledge, and at times, the patience of his teachers. His passion for science, and particularly, his extraordinary mathematical ability, had singled him out as a prodigy.

But Jack's minor celebrity was uncomfortable. He feared that all the foolish hubbub about "genius" was only making him an eyesore amongst his mates. When his teachers proposed to pass him ahead to University College Dublin, his mom and stepdad wisely vetoed the idea. They likewise declined the school's offer to let Conor, already an Irish national science fair winner, jump ahead to senior year. Neither of the boys objected.

As a compensation, Jack's physics teacher, Mr. Ryan, let him work by himself on advanced projects in the laboratory every morning. Conor was allowed to help. The headmistress, however, had imposed several formal restrictions: they could not, for example, attempt to build an atomic reactor or a liquid-fuel rocket. Otherwise they could do what they wished with the school's modest lab resources. Connolly was proud of its young scientists.

Jack had decided, with Conor's help, to design and build an ultra-lightweight, solar-powered trike.

A trike is a tiny aircraft that marries a three-wheeled carriage to a batlike wing. Trikes evolved out of inventors' attempts to create powered hang gliders. In the beginning the result was often a fatal disaster, because hang-glider wings are not strong enough to support the suspended weight of the trike frame and motorbike engine.

However, with the arrival of much stronger, reinforced wings and lighter-weight frames, trikes became a worldwide fad. Customized trikes with collapsible wings and aluminum engines are not much heavier than a canoe and are equally portable. Moreover, they can achieve airspeeds in excess of sixty miles per hour and stay aloft for several hours due to their combined characteristics of a glider and an airplane.

Now Jack was creating a third-generation trike that was a bold improvement on the best available commercial design. He had invented a hybrid engine that used solar cells on the wing to recharge small but powerful hydrogen batteries. Employing super-lightweight fullerene and magnesium components, he ruthlessly reduced the weight of the twin-seated carriage and wing without surrendering any structural strength. And aided by Conor's computer studies of bat and insect flight, he reshaped the double-surface wing for superior lift and stability.

The new trike was specifically designed for the needs of scientific expeditions and wilderness exploration. Its ultralight weight allowed it to carry more instrumentation, including a powerful real-time video camera in its nose pod that could be used to track birds in flight or wildlife on the ground. Interchangeable water skis and light alloy wheels allowed it to take off equally easily from water or land, and it could also be launched, like a hang glider, from a cliff. Finally, Jack's little plane could operate as a pilotless, remote-controlled drone, although it was less maneuverable in that mode.

Before its maiden flight, the design had to be submitted to the European Institute of Aeronautical Standards for engineering approval, and Jack had to go for a hearing before the Irish Aviation Authority. His physics teacher, Mr. Ryan, was coming by today to look over the forms with Jack.

4. MR. RYAN'S PROPOSAL

"How does it look, Jack?"

"Fine, Mr. Ryan. I've had to tinker with the alignment of the solar panels and add some new navigational software, but otherwise my trike is ready to fly to the North Pole."

"Not so fast," laughed Mr. Ryan. "You still need permission from the aviation board, and to be honest, I'm not optimistic about your chances. They might let you test it outside commercial airspace as a robot drone operated by radio control, but I don't think they will ever let you fly yourself. The design is too radical."

"I was afraid of that," said Jack glumly.

"Oh, cheer up," replied Mr. Ryan. "I have another proposal that I think you will find quite exciting."

"What's that?"

"Have you ever heard of the United Nations Science Challenge Summer School?"

"No."

"Nor, to be honest, had I, until last week." Mr. Ryan fumbled in his briefcase until he found a large manila envelope. "This is the application. Every year four kids are chosen by competition to spend a summer working at a scientific research station somewhere in the world. Often the sites are quite exciting: a deep-sea lab off the French Riviera, an atmospheric monitoring station on a Hawaiian volcano, a limestone cavern in Mexico, and so on."

"Sounds interesting," said Jack, only half paying attention.

"Yes, but guess where the winners are going next summer?"

"No idea," replied Jack, a little more attentively.

"Greenland. Tasiilaq, in East Greenland, actually. Professor Dansgaard's famous Arctic Natural History Institute. I think you went to Tasiilaq once with your father, didn't you?"

"Yes, when I was seven," said Jack, now full of interest.

"To cheer you up, I've brought you the application. I've already written you a letter of recommendation. You just need to complete the forms."

"Thanks, Mr. Ryan. I'd love to go back to Greenland, but this is wildlife and vegetation research, the kind of stuff Conor loves. I'm an aircraft inventor." Jack sounded defeated again.

"That's the whole point, Jack. The Institute's interested in new technology for the remote surveillance of Arctic ecosystems. Why, your trike—remotely controlled, of course—is the perfect tool for conducting a wildlife census or surveying tundra vegetation."

"That's true, Mr. Ryan." Jack was becoming enthused. "The trike could monitor herds of reindeer, track polar bear on the sea ice, even observe Arctic owls hunting hares at night. But it would break Conor's heart if I left him here for the summer."

"Well, take him along. The program accepts applications from student teams. And you and Conor have always worked together: let him handle the wildlife biology and you fiddle with the airborne technology. What do you say?"

"It's a fantastic idea—Conor would love to see Greenland."

"I knew I could cheer you up," smiled Mr. Ryan.

As Mr. Ryan had warned, the Irish Aviation Authority promptly turned down Jack's request to test his trike, although the European Institute of Aeronautics was so impressed with the novel design that, not realizing that he was only sixteen, they offered him a job.

The really good news arrived in early May. Actually it came in two parts: First came a thick parcel from the United Nations congratulating him and Conor on their acceptance to the science summer school. There were endless numbers of forms, releases, and medical questionnaires for their parents to fill out. Then a small letter arrived, postmarked Tasiilaq, from Professor Dansgaard himself. It was just a single sheet of paper neatly folded over. Inside there were five questions:

1. How many words are there in Greenlandic for snow?
2. What is a Tupilak?
3. What is a Piteraq?
4. What is Puisortoq?
5. Where are the mammoths?

Jack turned the paper over. On the back he wrote without hesitation:

Dear Professor Dansgaard:
Answers:
1. 46 words in West Greenlandic, 57 in Northwest Greenlandic, and 63 in East Greenlandic.
2. A Tupilak, in the old religious system of the Inuit, was a monstrous chimera fabricated by a sorcerer from the corpses of animals and men.[1]
3. Piteraq: an extremely dangerous, hurricane-velocity wind that arises when supercooled air cascades off the Inland Ice.
4. The most feared place in Greenland. An overhanging ice mountain that the Inuit avoid at all cost. One of the chief obstacles to the exploration of southeastern Greenland.*
5. In my dreams.

He posted the letter that afternoon.

The boys' summer scholarship to Greenland was a good local news story, and Jack and Conor got their photograph in the *Irish Times* along with a beaming Mr. Ryan and Conor's biology teacher, Mrs. O'Grady. Their friends were awed.

It was a long wait until the school term ended, but in mid-June they were finally free for their summer adventure. To reach East Greenland they first had to fly to Iceland; fortunately, a group of fanatic Bjork fans had chartered a direct flight from Dublin to Reykjavik, and Jack and Conor were invited to come along as guests. Amongst their extra luggage was the trike—now romantically renamed the "Icehawk"—folded up inside a torpedo-shaped aluminum tube that could be easily carried, like a lightweight canoe, by the two boys.

At Dublin Airport there was a big throng of school chums, Jack and Conor's tearful family, including their sister Roisin, and several reporters. In Reykjavik, after an easy two-hour flight, the Irish boys were stunned to be greeted at Keflavik Airport by the Icelandic Minister of Science and two busloads of curious local science students.

"Jeez, Conor," Jack whispered, "did Ireland win the World Cup?"

As it turned out, a local newspaper had done a Sunday supplement story on Jack's Icehawk, so the two brothers were being treated like heroic juvenile explorers setting off to face the unknown dangers of the Greenlandic ice.

All this commotion was becoming a little embarrassing. Jack had sworn to his Mom on his fossil collection that he and Conor would not undertake any foolhardy adventures like those that had gotten them in

---

*Jack later showed his brother the following passage on Puisortoq from Knud Rasmussen's field notes: "In the former days this was the most ill-famed passage. The glacier stands right out into the sea, and the Eskimos, who held the belief that the cold radiating from it froze even the bottom of the sea to ice, so that every few moments huge blocks of ice shot up without warning, were often held up there for weeks without being able to make further progress; and when at last they raced past in their *umiaks* they had not to say a word; one heard only the monotonous sound of the beat of the oars, and all women with small children had to lie in the bottom of the boat and cover their faces; for they believed that the mighty spirit of the glacier would smash the boat if a woman and child appeared to it."

so much trouble in the past. He assured her they would spend the summer snug inside the Dansgaard Institute classifying bugs.

"Do you intend to fly the Icehawk across the ice cap?" asked a reporter. Jack, who turned red, was glad his Mom didn't have access to Icelandic television.

"No," he emphasized, "my brother and I are just science students, not polar explorers. We'll spend the summer working with Professor Dansgaard."

"Well then, do you agree with Dansgaard's hypothesis? Do you think he could possibly be correct?"

The Icelanders all patiently awaited Jack's answer, but he didn't have a clue what they were talking about. He was beginning to feel a little panicky.

Conor saved the day. Pushing Jack gently aside, he smiled at the science students and reporters.

"Well, Dansgaard's Arctic refugia thesis is certainly provocative. We'll keep an open mind and report back at the end of the summer."

Conor sounded like Sherlock Holmes speaking about a mysterious crime, and the Icelanders were impressed by the answer.

Later, as the two brothers poached their shanks in the famous "Blue Lagoon" thermal lake, Jack asked Conor: "O.K., Mr. Know-It-All. What is all this about? Why's Dansgaard so controversial? What's a 'refugia thesis'?"

"Simple, my dear Watson," Conor replied, in his best Basil Rathbone accent. "'Refugia' is Latin for 'refuge.'"

"Refuge for what?" Jack was getting annoyed. "For mad scientists?"

"No, for species that have had to leave their traditional habitat because of climate change. For instance, during the last Ice Age most of the western United States was thickly forested. Then, after the end of the Ice Age, it became mainly desert. But some of the Ice Age tree species continue to survive near the top of the highest desert mountains. Those mountains are their refugia, and perhaps in a few thousand years, when the next Ice Age begins, the trees will slowly move down and reforest the desert."

"OK, so a 'refugia' is a hideout for an imperiled or nearly extinct species. But what has this to do with Greenland and Professor Dansgaard?"

"Well, Watson," Conor replied in even more flamboyant Rathbonese, "if you read natural history journals, you'd know that Professor Dansgaard believes that there are valleys in southeastern Greenland—so far unexplored—that might be refugia for certain plant species and also, possibly, for mammals."

"Mammals?"

"Yes, perhaps reindeer and polar wolves."[2]

"This is controversial?"

"Oh yes, at least until someone actually flies their trike over southeast Greenland and sees whether Prancer, Dancer, and Rudolph are frolicking in the valley below."

"Oh, god," Jack chuckled, "Dansgaard is searching for Santa Claus."

7. HELLO, JULIA

After two days in Iceland, boredom began to set in. Jack and Conor were more than ready for the exciting flight to East Greenland. They were also extremely curious about their fellow passenger.

Her name was Julia. She was, impressively, seventeen years old. She had bright blue eyes, long auburn hair, and an impish smile. She was wearing jeans and a tan jacket with a polar bear emblem.

"Hi! You must be the famous Irish boys," she said in an American accent.

Jack instantly became speechless.

"Conor, I presume?" Julia offered a firm handshake to Jack.

Jack couldn't move.

Conor kicked him in the leg, then said: "No, the tall silent one is Jack. I'm Conor the Barbarian. And you're Julia from the States."

"Yes, from New York, although I've also lived in France, Israel, and Argentina. And your brother, he's a deaf-mute?"

"Not really," Jack mumbled.

"He speaks," said Julia.

"*Bonjour*, Mademoiselle Julia."

Julia was delighted to have another French enthusiast to speak with.

"Now wait," Conor interrupted. "Don't leave me out of the conversation.

This summer is going to be enough of a linguistic challenge. Danish, Greenlandic, and now high school French. We need some ground rules."

"I agree," said Julia. "We'll speak English when we're all together."

"At least until we become fluent in Greenlandic," added Jack.

They all laughed. The three dialects of Greenlandic are amongst the most difficult languages in the world. (How do you pronounce, for instance, *"Qeqertarssuatsiaq"*—meaning "a large island?" And that's a simple word.)

"So anyway, Jack, how do you like all the newspaper publicity about your flying machine?" Julia was trying to tease him again.

"It's OK, but what do you do?" replied Jack, desperately trying to change the subject.

"*Ursus horribilis arcticus,*" replied Julia.

"Come again?" stumbled Jack.

"Polar bears, Watson," smiled Conor. "She won the U.S. National Science Fair last year with some wonderful research on hormonal imbalances in polar bears—isn't that right, Julia."

She put her arm around Conor. "What a sweetheart. Yes, I studied endocrine disruptors in the food chain of polar bears on Spitzbergen."

"You've been to Spitzbergen?" asked Jack, awed. The great desolate archipelago, owned by Norway, is almost as far north as the top of Greenland.

"Yes, I've spent two summers there. My mother is a marine biologist and my dad is a zoo curator, so I guess polar bears are in my genes."

And on your jeans too, Jack thought, as he noticed another polar bear insignia sewn on Julia's back pocket.

"So what's your racket, Conor?"

"Proboscideans."

Julia laughed. "Shouldn't you be spending the summer in Zimbabwe instead of Greenland? Or are you expecting to find some frozen mammoths?"

Conor smiled. "No such luck. I'm in charge of designing the animal recognition software for Jack's Icehawk. We've heard that Professor Dansgaard believes there may be reindeer hiding out in southeast Greenland."

"That's not what I heard," answered Julia with deliberate mystery.

"What's he looking for, then?" asked Jack.

"Something bigger than a reindeer and far more exotic. But I won't spoil your fun and tell you the rumor. You figure it out after you meet Professor Dansgaard."

"You're cruel," said Jack with a smirk.

"You guys have seen *Jurassic Park* too many times," giggled Conor, highly amused by the exchange. "Or maybe Conan Doyle's *Lost World.*"

"Wait and see," answered Julia, flashing her most mischievous grin.

EPISODE TWO: *Some Old Bones*

8. BACK TO THE ICE AGE

*T*he flight to Greenland was almost the same as Jack remembered from nine years earlier. The Fokker prop-jet took off from Reykjavik's City Airport on a cold clear morning. Three noses were pressed to the windows.

From the port side of the plane they had a glorious view of the great volcano Snaefellsjokull. Jack was the only one who had read Jules Verne's *A Journey to the Center of the Earth,* so he amused Conor and Julia with an account of how the crater on the top of Snaefellsjokull was actually the secret entrance to the earth's interior. He even remembered the famous note from Arne Saknussemm:

> *Descend into the crater of Yocull of Snaeffels,*
> *Which the shade of Scartaris caresses,*
> *Before the kalends of July, audacious traveller*
> *And you will reach the centre of the earth. I did.*[3]

Julia laughed. "I wonder if we will have some amazing adventure, or just spend the summer being eaten by arctic mosquitoes?"

"Who knows," Jack replied, "maybe we'll discover a colony of lost Vikings."

"Or find the frozen carcass of an ancient mammoth," added Conor.

"I'd settle for a few polar bears," sighed Julia, as she fingered the polar bear amulet she wore around her neck.

After about ten minutes, Iceland had receded over the horizon and their plane had climbed above the thick cloud layer that perpetually covers the Denmark Strait between Iceland and Greenland.

Jack reassured Conor and Julia, however, that the sky was usually clear over the Greenland coast itself.

Sure enough, just after the pilot told the solitary flight attendant to prepare for landing, the clouds suddenly yielded to bright sunshine and a view of the magnificent islands that guard Ammassalik Fjord. Conor let out an exclamation of astonishment and pleasure, just as Jack had years before. Julia, an old pro in the Arctic, merely beamed.

The airport on Kulusuk Island was gravel, having been built by the

Americans during World War II, but the rugged little Fokker landed without a bump. Jack wanted to show Conor the polar bear pelts inside the tiny terminal, but the helicopter to take them to Tasiilaq was already waiting.

The efficient ground crew unloaded their gear onto a small flatbed truck and drove them across to the helicopter pad. Julia winked at Jack: one of the crewmen had a copy of *Mad Magazine* in his back pocket.

The helicopter pilot—a handsome Greenlander—smiled when the kids introduced themselves, but then frowned when he saw the pile of gear the young scientists were proposing to ferry to Tasiilaq.

"What's that?" he asked, eyeing the tube containing the Icehawk.

"It's my airplane, or rather, trike. Of course, it needs to be assembled," replied Jack.

"You mean it's a toy," corrected the pilot.

"No, it's real. Full-sized. I could fly from here to Tasiilaq if I wanted to."

The pilot furrowed his eyebrows again and walked over to the trike. He pushed it with both hands as if expecting it to be extremely heavy, and it easily gave way.

"Airplane, sure . . . any day," he sniggered. Then he frowned at Jack and said something unmentionable in Greenlandic.

A few minutes later the gear was neatly stowed, although with no room to spare, and the helicopter effortlessly lifted into pale blue sky.

Although it was late June, there were still large plates of milky sea ice. Icebergs were too numerous to count, as were the jagged-edged peaks: scores of Matterhorns with small outlet glaciers nestled between them. In the distance they could see the towering edge of the Inland Ice itself.

It was an overwhelming vista. They were traveling not so much in space as in time, returning to an Ice Age world.

9. LAST FLOWERS ON EARTH

Jack had done some research and had jotted down a few notes in his journal:

Tasiilaq, known to the Danes as Ammassalik, is the major community in East Greenland. Indeed, it is the only real town along 2,500 kilometers of the most rugged, inaccessible, but magnificent coast on earth.

There were, to be sure, five smaller villages outside of Tasiilaq on the Ammassalik and Sermilik Fjords, as well as the isolated hunting village of Ittoqqoortoormiit, seven hundred miles to the North. But that was all—north of Ittoqqoortoormiit there was only a handful of elite Danish ski patrol officers patrolling the world's largest wilderness preserve. And oddly, no human beings at all lived south of Tasiilaq in southeastern Greenland. Indeed, some parts of that southern coast—especially its inland valleys—had barely been explored. (Jack wrote: "Ask Dansgaard why?")

For two thousand years the mountains of East Greenland had been a tantalizing mirage to European sailors. They were first seen by a lost Greek, then by Erik the Red, the Viking colonizer of western Greenland. His descendants all saw them on their return voyages from Iceland, as did thousands of later English, Dutch, and Norwegian whalers. No European set foot in the Ammassalik area until 1884, when the Danish naval lieutenant Gustav Holm had himself rowed up the southeast coast by a stout crew of west coast Inuit women.

Holm was lucky. The East Greenland Current is the world's most formidable conveyor belt of ice. Trying to make landfall in East Greenland is impossible ten months out of every year, and it's very dangerous even in August. Fridtjof Nansen, the great Norwegian explorer who was the first to cross the Inland Ice, got within a mile offshore of Tasiilaq and tried to land in a whaleboat. The ice, however, blocked his path, and the powerful current swept him south for nearly four hundred miles until he could finally struggle ashore.

When the East Greenlanders met Lieutenant Holm in 1884, they thought he was a *tupilak*, a monster made by a sorcerer, because they had been isolated from other Inuit for almost a thousand years and thought they lived alone on an ice planet. There were only four hundred of them, the majority of whom lived in Tasiilaq.

After a few months Holm managed to learn a few words of Greenlandic. Pointing to a small flower on the coastline where Tasiilaq meets the ocean, he said "flower." His Greenlandic guide said, "Yes, the last flowers on earth."

"What will the Greenlanders think of us?" Jack wondered aloud as the pilot maneuvered the helicopter down to the ground.

At exactly the same moment, Qavigarssuag—"Qav" for short—was standing by the helicopter pad asking himself: "What will my three summer friends be like?"

The helicopter slowly eased into the landing circle amidst a small whirlwind of snow and debris. After the rotor finally stopped, the pilot opened the door for the trio. They looked around to see what kind of reception committee had come to greet them. No one knew exactly what Dr. Dansgaard looked like, and they were consumed with curiosity.

"Hi, there. Jack, Conor, and Julia, I presume."

The words were spoken by an Inuit boy, about Conor's height and age, with a broad face that framed a huge smile and twinkling eyes. Surprisingly, he had red hair. His English was impeccable, although spoken with a slight burr.

Conor was terrified to reply: how do you pronounce: Qavigarsuag?

"Just call me Qav—pronounced like "Kav"—it's my nickname. We'll deal with proper Greenlandic names later," said the boy as everyone shook hands.

"Is Dr. Dansgaard here?" Julia asked.

Qav giggled. "No, but don't feel offended. Our great doctor was up all night working in the laboratory. You'll see him shortly. Here, let me help you with your gear."

Qav discreetly appraised his new mates. Jack was medium height with brown hair and freckle-dappled cheeks. He looked studious, kind, and responsible. Conor was sandy-haired with a slightly mischievous grin. Although shorter than his brother, he had the physique of a serious gymnast or rock climber. Surprisingly, so did Julia, who was slender but muscular, with a dancer's poise. "Good," Qav thought to himself, "at least two genuine outdoor types."

They piled the small mountain of luggage as well as the Icehawk in the back of a beat-up Land Rover. Tasiilaq had exactly two miles of paved road, with perhaps seven of gravel.

Qav started the engine. "Do you drive, Conor?"

"Boy, I wish I could, but I'm only thirteen. How old are you, Qav?"

"Thirteen, and I have been driving since I was ten."

Conor was impressed.

They slowly pulled out of the tiny airport and began the bumpy ride into Tasiilaq, a village of steep hills and seemingly steeper valleys.

"What does your name mean, Qav?" Jack asked.

"Son of the hunter."

"So, your dad is a seal hunter?"

Qav giggled again. "Not really. He's a doctor. East Greenland's flying doctor. He travels by helicopter and in the winter by dog team to the outlying hunting camps to take care of the sick. My mom's a schoolteacher; she's Scottish."

"But Qav, why then aren't you named 'son of doctor'?" asked Julia, a stickler for precision.

"Because my name actually refers to my grandfather, who is a hunter. In fact, he is the last of the old school. He lives alone far up the fjord and still stalks seal in a kayak. But you will hear loads more about him later. When they were young, he and Dansgaard spent years together exploring the East Coast."

Qav went on to explain that he was the fourth member of the summer team. He was selected not because he was a local, but rather because he had published an award-winning paper on the computer modeling of arctic ecosystems. Qav had just returned to Tasiilaq from Copenhagen, where he was attending one of the most prestigious secondary schools in Scandinavia.

"So I've been away all winter."

"Were you homesick?" asked Conor, secretly wondering how he would feel a week from now.

"All the time, although I live with a wonderful family in Denmark. I missed my parents, my little sister, even the howling of our sled dogs. But my grandfather sends dreams to comfort me when I am lonely."

"Sends dreams?" Julia sounded skeptical. The Land Rover slowed for a huge pothole.

Qav laughed. "I know it doesn't sound very scientific, but yes, my grandfather sends me wonderful dreams, full of messages from my family and images of Greenland."

"Maybe you should be called 'son of the wizard,'" said Julia, still unconvinced.

Qav was silent for a moment, then he smiled again. "Funny you should say that. My grandfather *is* actually a bit of a wizard. It runs in the family. You see, his grandfather was the legendary Aua, the most famous of the Ammassalik sorcerers. When all the rest of the East Greenlanders converted to Christianity in the 1890s, Aua alone refused. He took his kayak and disappeared in the south."

"Was he ever heard of again?" asked Conor, fascinated.

"Oh yes, my grandfather talks to him all the time," Qav replied, deadpan.

Julia started to protest, but Jack changed the subject.

"Look, the Museum and the research station!"

"Oh, I forgot, you've been here before," said Qav.

"Yes, and I'm very excited to be back. And to be with my brother and two good friends."

Both Qav and Julia were touched. Conor was, too, although he was already thinking to himself: "When Jack is out picking flowers with Julia, maybe Qav will teach me to drive the Land Rover."

11. MYSTERY DOG

Tasiilaq was a picturesque town sprawled across roller-coaster hills overlooking a small dock and tiny fishing harbor. The brightly painted two-story houses had steeply pitched roofs with winter entrances on the second floor. Between the houses were pretty patches of summer flowers, as well as fish drying racks, old boats, and yesterday's sleds.

Dogs and kids seemed to rule Tasiilaq. The unbuilt parts of town were a huge outdoor kennel for magnificent-looking Greenlandic huskies. They were tethered by long chains to iron stakes and fed once a day with buckets of fish offal. Huskies have a complicated social order. Summer was a season of recouping strength for the fierce Fall competitions that sorted out sled team hierarchies. These were the ancient rituals of the wolf pack.

But Tasiilaq's kids, as the summer scientists would quickly discover, lived in two worlds. When they weren't fishing off the little bridge that crossed the creek, they were skateboarding suicidally down the steep street in front of the post office. They played prehistoric games and challenged each other with thousand-year-old riddles, but they also loved Nintendo, Hong Kong kung fu videos, surfing the Internet, and competitive kayaking.

Qav patiently coaxed the wheezing Land Rover up the near-vertical street by the post office. As skateboarders zoomed by, some waved at him or shouted greetings. Just beyond the crest of the hill was the Arctic Natural History Institute.

Its director was waiting outside the museum door.

Dr. Dansgaard was a towering old Viking, perhaps six-foot-four, with a shock of white hair, a great eagle's beak of a nose, and eyes the ultramarine of glacial ice. He was wearing a moth-eaten gray sweater, the kind that Icelandic fishermen prefer, but incongruously, his feet were in sandals. At his side was a great golden dog.

"Welcome to Tasiilaq," said Dansgaard, in thickly accented English. "*Qanoq ateqarpit?* (What are your names?)," he asked.

"I'm Jack. And this is Julia and my brother Conor."

"So you speak Greenlandic, young man?"

Jack blushed. "Maybe ten words."

Dansgaard laughed. "Don't worry. Qav will teach you at least ten more in the course of summer."

"What a beautiful dog." Julia said.

"Yes, and what a mysterious dog," replied Dansgaard. "Let me introduce Anori."

Anori calmly scrutinized each of the kids. Then he barked what might be construed as a greeting.

"He came out of the fog one day while I was collecting specimens two hundred miles south of here. He has been by my side ever since."

"But no one lives along the southeast coast," said Jack, puzzled.

"Precisely. That is why he is a mystery dog." Dansgaard focused his eyes sharply on Qav. "Tell our newcomers why Anori is so exceptional."

Qav turned to face the other three. "There are three thousand sled dogs in Tasiilaq. None of them approaches Anori's size or approximates his golden color. And he barks. Greenlandic huskies can't bark. They only howl."

"Perhaps someone brought him from Europe or another part of the Arctic," suggested Julia.

"Unlikely," Qav replied. "All of our sled dogs are the direct descendants of those our ancestors brought when they came to Greenland more than a thousand years ago. To preserve their lineage, it is against the law to bring dogs into Greenland."

"So where did he come from?" asked Conor.

"My grandfather says that he is his grandfather's dog. The dog of Aua, the sorcerer. 'Anori' means 'wind.'"

As Julia rolled her eyes in disbelief, Jack and Conor stared at each other, and Qav looked embarrassed.

Dr. Dansgaard fixed his gaze on Julia. "So, my dear, you don't believe in sorcery or 150-year-old dogs?"

She was defiant. "No, I am afraid I don't. After all," she emphasized, "we are here as scientists."

Dansgaard put his arm around her. "Of course, my dear, science. So let me show you your summer home."

Dansgaard led them up the stone stairway to the Institute. Conor hung back so he could whisper into Qav's ear. "Qav, is there something strange going on here?"

Qav whispered back, "This is Greenland, Conor. There are mysteries everywhere. Enjoy."

12. COUNTING REINDEER

The Institute and its attached public museum were in a beautiful old building hewn of driftwood and imported cedar on a platform of pre-Cambrian gneiss quarried from a nearby hill; it consisted of two exhibit rooms, a small theater, and an office. Outside, a small sign advised visitors that the facility was jointly supported by the National Museum of Greenland and the Danish Polar Center. There were also two laboratories, both in prefabricated buildings from the former American base at Kuummit, up Ammassalik Fjord—one winter in the 1950s the abandoned buildings were hauled by dog teams forty miles across the ice to Tasiilaq.

One of the buildings—what Americans call a "Quonset hut" and the British a "Nissan hut"—was Dr. Dansgaard's workroom. He was very secretive about what he did inside, brushing off questions with: "Oh, just some research on some old bones I found." The kids jokingly called it "Frankenstein's Lab." It was locked and guarded by Anori, the mystery dog.

The other building was where the kids were to work. Qav and Jack would collaborate on readying the Icehawk to fly as pilotless drone, while Conor and Julia were to organize a census of the small reindeer (caribou) herd that still lived north of Tasiilaq in a long beautiful valley of glacial lakes and streams known as Kuugarmitt Aqqutaat.

The plan was for all four of them to conduct a two-day reindeer count on the ground, estimating the age and sex of the animals. Then, when the Icehawk was ready, they would duplicate the census from the air, using the nose-mounted videocam. The difference between the two would enable Dansgaard to estimate the size of the local reindeer herd, as well as other wildlife populations, including musk oxen, that he had previously counted from the ground.

At least that was the official work program. But in Greenland the unexpected always seemed to happen.

13.   A SURPRISE FOR CONOR

A week later the kids were camped outside of Kuugarmitt, a tiny settlement of just three homes and two extended families at the northern end of the reindeer valley, a long day's boat ride from Tasiilaq. Jack and Qav had interrupted their work on the Icehawk to help Conor and Julia count reindeer.

"OK, gang," said Julia. "Here's the plan. Qav and Conor will walk south along the left side of the valley, keeping high enough on the slope not to panic the reindeer. They'll record everything on one of these videocams. Jack and I will do the same thing on the right side of the valley. We'll converge and meet at the final and largest lake. It should take about three or four hours."

The morning, which started chilly and wet, brightened as they climbed higher in the valley. After two hours Qav and Conor had yet to see a single reindeer. They were deep inside a great trough between two immense, glacier-covered mountain ranges. There were gorgeous patches of flowers and even some dwarf willows by the stream, but the valley otherwise seemed utterly lifeless. It was so silent that when Conor coughed, it echoed like a gunshot.

"So are these reindeer invisible . . ." Conor started to ask, when Qav suddenly put his hand to his mouth.

"Shhhh."

Ahead of them, frozen like little statues, were about a half-dozen Greenlandic caribou, two does and four or five fawns. Conor aimed his videocamera as the reindeer remained motionless. Then Qav started to move forward, as silently as he could, but a small twig snapped under his foot, the noise magnified by the valley's magical sound chamber.

The reindeer were gone in an instant. "Wow," said Conor.

"Yeah, wow," replied Qav. They continued up the valley, trying to tread as softly as possible.

An hour later, having seen no more reindeer, they arrived at their rendezvous spot; a large but shallow lake surrounded by huge boulders and patches of marsh with clouds of bugs overhead. The boys found a smooth dry rock a safe distance from the swarming gnats and mosquitoes. They were famished, so they decided not to wait for Julia and Jack to begin lunch.

Conor sat facing Qav. "Here, Qav, try a bite of this."

Suddenly Qav's face was illuminated by a mysterious smile. Puzzled, Conor whispered: "Do you see more reindeer?"

"Just turn around," Qav replied, with a twinkle in his eye.

Conor turned his head and gasped. Towering over him was a fierce-looking old man in a parka. He was carrying an enormous iron-tipped spear. He leaned his face down close to Conor's, and making a hideous expression, he growled: "Grrrrr!"

Conor fell over backwards as Qav laughed hysterically.

"Meet my grandad, Conor. This is Anaq."

"*Inuugujoq. Halluu*," said the old man, putting his hand gently on Conor's shoulder.

"Grandad only speaks Greenlandic. He says hello and apologizes for scaring you."

"*Halluu*," Conor replied. Having recovered from his fright, he was delighted to meet Qav's legendary grandfather.

Qav and his grandfather conversed for a few minutes. Anaq suddenly laughed, and then Qav, looking embarrassed, shook his head and giggled as well.

"What did he say?" Conor asked.

"He wanted to know what we were doing here, and I told him we were counting reindeer. He says we should have just asked him: there are forty-eight caribou, give or take a few fawns."

"How does he know that?"

"Believe me, his count is correct. He's an old hunter and has known this reindeer herd for a lifetime."

Just then, Jack and Julia walked up. They were also thrilled to meet Qav's grandfather.

Jack decided to take some baby steps in speaking Greenlandic. "Please," he haltingly asked Anaq, "tell us your story."

The old man smiled and spoke to Qav, who translated: "Grandfather says, first a cup of tea, please, then he'll be happy to spin a yarn or two."

14. AN UNMENTIONABLE PLACE

Conor made the tea while the others sat in a semicircle around Anaq. Qav translated rapidly as his grandfather spoke.

Anaq was nearly seventy-eight years old but looked twenty-five years younger. He had a handsome, weather-furrowed face, narrower than most Inuit men, with a walrus-like moustache and intense dark eyes. He was the last of the *piniartorssuaqs*, the traditional hunters.

He had outlived three wives. One perished of pneumonia, another in childbirth, while the third, Qav's grandmother, had died peacefully of old age a few years before. After her death, Anaq chose to live alone on a tiny island near one of the great glaciers that calve icebergs into Ammassalik Fjord.

Hunters today preferred speedboats and rifles, but Anaq still used a skin-covered kayak and a spear. His spearhead had been chipped off, centuries before, from the sacred meteorite that the American explorer

Peary later stole from Cape York in Northwest Greenland. Julia remembered seeing it in the entrance hall of the American Museum of Natural History in New York. Anaq had bartered three polar bear pelts to a Dane for the small piece of the extraterrestrial metal believed by Greenlanders to possess great talismanic powers.[4]

Anaq told them how, as a small boy, he had met Knud Rasmussen, Greenland's national hero. Rasmussen led the famous Thule expeditions in the 1920s that reestablished contact between Greenlanders and their Inuit relatives throughout the Arctic. During his visit to Ammassalik in 1934, however, he became fatally ill. Danish doctors said he died of salmonella, but Anaq was sure he had been poisoned by a local hunter who was jealous of Rasmussen's fame.

Anaq also talked about thrilling adventures during World War II when he had been part of the celebrated Ski Patrol, made up of ten Inuit hunters and four Danish explorers. The Allies vitally depended on this tiny unit to counter persistent German efforts to establish weather stations on the east coast of Greenland. The winds in the high latitudes flow west to east, so Greenland's weather is Northern Europe's two days ahead. The Germans desperately wanted this advanced weather information to help plan battles and air attacks.[5]

Anaq and his comrades tracked a Nazi landing party for five hundred miles before engaging them in a brief battle near Denmarkshavn in the far northeast. The Nazi commandoes were no match for Greenlandic hunters. Two of the Germans were killed, and the rest were captured. An American general gave Anaq a medal and a brand new metal boat, which he traded for his second wife. (Julia frowned.)

After the war, Anaq became guide and inseparable companion to the young Dr. Dansgaard. They explored and collected specimens together for eight seasons in the late 1950s and early 1960s.

"Where did you go?" Conor asked, wide-eyed.

"Oh, everywhere. All the way north to Independence Fjord and Peary Land. Also to seldom visited, or sometimes unexplored parts of Lamberts Land, King Oscar's Fjord, and the Stauning Alps. Twice onto the Inland Ice. And also to places where humans are not supposed to go."

"What do you mean?" asked Jack nervously.

Anaq narrowed his eyes and chose his words carefully. "Two hundred miles south of Ammassalik, the Inland Ice directly meets the ocean. It is an ice wall nearly three hundred meters high. To pass by this place—whose name can't be mentioned—is to kiss death."

Jack knew he was speaking about the dreaded Puisortoq: the place of screaming ice. By tradition East Greenlanders are forbidden to ever speak its name, yet somehow their children learn of it.

"But didn't early explorers like Holm and Nansen pass it safely?" asked Jack.

Anaq focused on Jack. "Yes, and twice Dansgaard and I passed by the hideous cliff of ice without incident."

"So this place-whose-name-we-can't-say isn't so dangerous after all?" asked Julia cheerfully.

"The third time we returned to Ammassalik . . ." Anaq stopped in the middle of his sentence. He had a pained expression, like that of older people when they remember a long-dead wife or child.

"Dansgaard had a young wife. She was of our people, from Nuuk on the west coast. She was happy and brave and 'modern.' Yes, 'modern,' like Dansgaard used to be, and you children are. She didn't believe in any of the old Inuit wisdom—she called it 'superstition.'"

"What happened?" asked Jack.

"Dansgaard's wife came with us the third time we tempted the ice. A berg broke off from the submerged base of the glacier, and suddenly it erupted from the sea in front of us. It was immense, maybe thirty meters high. We were swamped by a huge wave."

Everyone was silent for a long minute or so.

"I managed to save Dansgaard, although he was unconscious for minutes, but we never saw his wife again or ever found her body."

"Why did you keep returning to that unmentionable dangerous place?" asked Conor.

Anaq narrowed his eyes. "Perhaps we had been enchanted by a sorcerer. Or simply seduced by the idea of fame. But we were looking for something just south of the ice cliffs."

"Have you ever returned?" It was Qav's turn to ask a question.

"To that inhuman, evil place?" Anaq laughed bitterly. "I've spent forty years trying to forget the horror of what happened there. But this winter I went back with Dansgaard."

"Grandfather, are you serious?" Qav was shocked. "You might have been killed."

Anaq stared at his beloved grandson. "I'm very old, Qav, all my children and grandchildren thrive. Dansgaard is an old friend. Something, perhaps the sad memory of his young wife, lured him back. I went with him. We traveled by dogsleds."

"But wait, excuse me, I'm even more confused than Conor," said Julia. "Where exactly did you return to? What is this place south of the killer ice?"

Anaq suddenly had the beatific smile of a zen master or prophet. He looked directly and intensely at Julia, as if he were studying her very soul. She trembled slightly.

"Ah, to the place of the Ancients. To a valley like none other in Greenland or in this whole world, where time has stopped."

"But what did you find there, Grandfather?" Qav asked urgently.

Anaq stroked his head. "Qav, I swore to Dansgaard never to tell what we've seen. Old hunters keep their word."

"But please!!!" implored all four of the kids. They were desperate with curiosity.

Anaq smiled. "Has Dansgaard showed you the bones?"

"You mean the bones in his laboratory?" asked Jack.

"Yes, the bones we brought back this winter."

"No, he mentioned them once, but he doesn't allow us near his laboratory."

"It is guarded by the great dog?"

"Yes."

"Well, I can't say anything more than this: The secret is in those bones. And the great dog likes raw fish. Now, this old man must say goodnight. *Kasuuta!*"

Anaq started to walk off, then he turned sharply and said something in Julia's direction. Qav translated: "Grandfather says, 'sweet dreams.'"

15. BLUE BEARS

Anaq camped just out of sight of the kids. Even though it was nine or ten in the evening, it was still bright: in early July it really never got fully dark in the far north. Instead, a kind of twilight settled in, starting about one in the morning and lasting only two or three hours.

Julia and Qav were able to simply close their eyes and doze off, but Jack and Conor, still unused to sleeping in the light, stayed up half the night talking to each other about the mysterious bones. They simply had to find a way to sneak into Dansgaard's lab, even at risk of being caught and possibly being sent home.

Meanwhile, Julia was fast asleep in her down sleeping bag. She was dreaming that she was out on the pack ice, so far out that the shore was no longer visible, just pressure ridges and ice buckled into strange forms. The whole world was brilliantly white: the ice, her gloves, the sky, her parka, everything. Then, suddenly, she saw a blue dot coming towards her, and it was growing larger. It was, unbelievably, a bear cub—a bright blue polar bear cub. She laughed in her sleep and turned over.

In the morning, Jack and Conor were still snoring in their sleeping bags as Qav boiled some tea and talked with his grandfather, who was packed and ready to leave. Julia raised her head from the sleeping bag and rubbed her eyes.

"Good morning, pretty girl from America," said old Anaq. "Did you like your blue bear?"

Julia's jaw dropped, and Anaq laughed. He hugged Qav, rubbed his nose Inuit-style, and walked off briskly, as if he were a young man and not almost an Ancient himself.

Julia was still in shock, too paralyzed to move. She might, after all, have to adjust some of her ideas.

16. THE BREAK-IN

Back in Tasiilaq, Jack and Conor revealed their plan to Qav and Julia: They were going to sneak into Dansgaard's lab while he was asleep. They would follow Anaq's advice and distract the great yellow dog with

a big meal. Jack was confident he could finesse the lock open.

Julia easily thought of a dozen reasons for not going along with the plan, everything from hurting Dansgaard's feelings to being expelled in disgrace from the summer program. On the other hand, she was just as consumed with curiosity as the others, so the break-in was agreed upon.

They carefully plotted for nearly a week. Then, on a Sunday night, just a little after midnight, when they were sure Dansgaard was at home asleep, they gingerly approached his lab. The yellow dog was napping in front of the door. As Jack and Conor walked closer, Anori awoke and stood up—not menacingly, but impressively. He just stood there, blocking the door and eyeing the boys curiously. At that moment Qav and Julia appeared, carrying a huge plate of fresh mackerel and halibut. The great dog instantly nudged Jack and Conor aside and ran to the plate. He didn't even turn to look as the kids rushed the door, which, amazingly, wasn't locked.

The lab was full of sophisticated but generally secondhand equipment, including a sprawling carbon-14 dating apparatus that could tell the age, within a decade or two, of ancient organic material like cross-sections of trees or fragments of bone. It was the only such lab setup in Greenland, or for that matter, in the entire Arctic.

The bones, carefully arranged on a huge work table, were massive and white. Only Conor instantly recognized what they were.

Conor seemed to be in some kind of strange trance. He was doing a little jig and smiling as if he had won the lottery. Jack had never seen his little brother acting more odd.

"For heavens' sake, Conor, what's up? Have you gone bonkers?"

"No, not at all. But let me show you what Santa Claus—or, rather, Dr. Dansgaard—has brought me for Christmas. These are mammoth bones, Jack. Mammoth bones."

Jack now understood his brother's excitement—nothing would make Conor happier than a skeleton of his favorite prehistoric creature. He'd been studying mastodons and mammoths for years, and he probably knew as much about them as senior scientists five times his age. But why the mystery? Why hadn't Dansgaard simply shared his discovery?

"Here, let me show you around." Conor had switched on an overhead light and began a brilliant impromptu lecture on the dead mammoth. ". . . and by the size and concavity of this joint, we can tell that this was a full-grown, probably male, mammoth, but of a pygmy subspecies. Just like in your dream, Jack."

"Well done, Conor." A chill went up four spines as the kids recognized Dr. Dansgaard's voice. He was in the back of the room with the great dog, now well fed, panting at his side. His expression was fiercesome, to say the least.

"Doctor, please let me explain . . ." started Jack. "No, doctor, it was my fault . . ." interrupted Qav. "Actually, I'm to blame . . ." interjected Julia. The kids were trembling.

Dansgaard's face grew even darker, like a thundercloud about to discharge a deadly bolt of lightning. "Do you know what the penalty is for breaking into my lab?" he said in his most menacing voice.

Jack could feel his knees shaking.

Then, suddenly, the cloud dissipated and Dansgaard nearly collapsed in laughter. Even his dog seemed to be laughing. The kids were totally disoriented. Were they in trouble, or not?

Dansgaard collected himself. "Science is the child of curiosity, is it not?" he asked Qav.

"Yes, I think so," offered Qav hesitantly.

"Of course it is. And any good scientist will follow its path regardless. So to test you, I planted a first-class mystery in front of you and waited to see how you all would react. You've passed your midterm, so to speak, and Conor, I'm giving you an A-plus for your lecture on mammoth anatomy."

The kids let out a collective gasp of relief. Julia, however, seemed slightly disappointed.

"So, there really isn't a mystery after all?" she asked.

Dansgaard became more serious. "No, I didn't say that. In fact, there is a mystery in this room probably beyond your imagination, as it once was beyond mine. You have fifteen minutes to tell me what that mystery is, or I'll lock the door and we'll speak no more of it, ever." Dansgaard sat down and petted the dog.

The kids were stupefied. Nothing could be worse than having come so close to the mystery and then not find it.

"Conor," Jack whispered, "what's strange about the bones? Do you see anything unusual?"

"No . . ." stuttered Conor, "they are extremely well preserved, almost as if the mammoth died yesterday, but nothing else is unusual. Pygmy mammoths and mastodons were quite common toward the end of the Ice Age when their populations became confined to smaller ecologies: islands in the Mediterranean and off California, on the

Kalmyra Peninsula of Siberia, and so on. Great bones, but not especially mysterious."[6]

"OK, gang." Julia again took command. "The mystery must be elsewhere in the lab. Let's fan out and look. Check all the lab notebooks and the data. There must be a clue."

The kids pored through dozens of notebooks and charts, looking for anything that might provide a last-minute clue.

"Seven minutes left," Dansgaard said with a cruel grin.

The strange scavenger hunt became more frenetic. What were they looking for?

"Two minutes. You are almost out of luck." Dansgaard was even crueler.

Time was almost up when Conor suddenly shouted: "This can't be right! No, I don't believe this! Dr. Dansgaard, what are you up to here? Have you falsified a lab book to taunt us?" Conor was irked.

Dansgaard walked over to him. He gently took the notebook, patted Conor on the shoulder, and told everyone to sit down. The yellow dog resumed guarding the door.

17. AN IMPOSSIBLE DATE

"Conor again is ahead of all of you. I must apologize for treating this as a game. He is right to be upset. Before I attempt to give you an explanation, scientific or otherwise, I will let Conor tell you what he found in the lab book."

Conor stood up, still obviously annoyed. "This is the notebook for the carbon-14 test sequence. It records various kinds of data, but the pertinent column is the last one. This is the adjusted age of different specimens of old wood and bone that Dr. Dansgaard has been testing."

Conor passed the book around and waited until it was returned to him. "Look at this entry, for example. It is a piece of mammoth ivory, not from the specimen on the table, but from another, smaller piece of tusk. The carbon-14 dating shows it to be from 9,800 years before present."

"But that's not exceptional," interrupted Julia.

"No, it's not," said Conor. "Just what you would expect. Mammoths only lived in Greenland for a short time, if at all. During the glacial maximum, the ice sheet covered everything. There was only a brief window of time—maybe 2,000 years—during which there was enough bare surface and vegetation for mammoths to cross to Greenland from Baffin Island. For reasons we don't completely understand, maybe because of overhunting by humans or vegetation change or both, they became extinct soon after, in the Canadian Arctic by about 7500 B.C., although on isolated Wrangel Island in the Bering Sea they survived until 1700 B.C."

"Enough, enough!" said Qav, uncharacteristically agitated. "Stop the lecture and get to the point."

Conor smiled triumphantly. "OK, guys, here's the punchline: This is the column that dates a sample of the mammoth bones on the table. What date would you expect?"

"Somewhere between 10,000 and 8,000 years ago, or in the wildest possible scenario, maybe 4,000 years ago, like the Wrangel mammoths." Julia was speaking in her most cool and mature voice.

"Well, for some reason which I can't guess, Dr. Dansgaard has entered a very different date."

"Tell us, for Pete's sake," shouted Jack. Both he and Qav were on their feet now.

"Unless Dr. Dansgaard made a simple clerical error, the dating of these bones shows that the animal died sometime in the last two years. A pygmy wooly mammoth, DOA, sometime before my twelfth or eleventh birthday." Conor sat down.

"That's daft," said Jack. "Crazy," said Julia. "Odd," said Qav. Then they all turned and stared at Dr. Dansgaard.

He coughed and cleared his throat. "Compliments again to Conor, he has a first-class forensic mind. But, Conor, please take another look at my notebook. Observe the pages immediately following this entry."

Conor opened the notebook and turned through several more pages of data. His brow furrowed. "But Doctor, according to this, you tested and retested the sample more than two dozen times. Your procedure is completely orthodox: extracting and purifying the bone collagen, then using a liquid scintillation counter for dating. And—here on this other page—you took some new collagen samples and tested them over again as well."

"Yes?" said Dansgaard.

"And the dating always turns out the same. Could your rather elderly apparatus be malfunctioning?"

"No, I think not," replied Dansgaard. "I doubled-checked the calibration with Glasgow University–dated samples that are used in all labs for quality control as well as with other specimens of mammoth and mastodon bone. Those all produced dates in conformity with scientific orthodoxy. Only this skeleton is different. Now, all of you, come here."

Dansgaard walked over to the large Zeiss stereoscopic microscope. A tiny cross-section of bone was under the lens. "Julia, take a look at this."

Julia peered into the microscope. She gasped. Then Conor took a look—a second gasp.

Jack and Qav stared for ages at the sample but didn't have a clue about what they were supposed to see.

"Cell tissue, recently dead," said Julia. "What you would find in the bone of the steak you ate last night, but not in ancient bones, because bacteria completely decompose the tissue after a few years. This bone is newly dead. Modern. Yesterday, almost." Julia looked dazed.

Conor was calmer. "OK, Dr. Dansgaard, we accept your evidence. But what is your explanation? Have you managed to insert mammoth DNA in the egg of a modern Indian elephant and produce clonal offspring? Is this a Frankenstein genetics experiment? Pleistocene Park?"

Conor was thinking about the highly publicized but so far unsuccessful attempts by the Japanese scientist Kazufumi Goto to clone "neo-mammoths" using ancient tissue retrieved from the Siberian permafrost.[7]

Dansgaard frowned.

"Conor, do you see the apparatus in this laboratory to undertake the cloning of a mammoth, even if such a procedure were possible? Of course not. Only a few labs in the world, perhaps only in Tokyo, Cambridge, and Berkeley, would have the capability. You know that."

"True," said Conor, suddenly very puzzled and a bit weary. "But what then? The last mammoths died off in the early Bronze Age. And mammoth remains have never been found in Greenland, except as items of trade ivory originating in Canada."

"Please, Dr. Dansgaard," Julia piped in. "We've followed the trail you prepared for us and we've passed all your tests. Now it is time to tell us the full story."

The kids took their seats again. "This may be a long night," Dansgaard warned, as he pulled his pipe out of his pocket. The great dog was curled at his feet.

EPISODE THREE: *Dansgaard's Secret*

"*A*ll this started with the Yanks in the mid-1950s." Dansgaard lit his pipe. "At that time, my interest was primarily in the unexplored tracts of the Northeast. Along that coast are countless archaeological sites testifying to the migration of Qav's ancestors around the northern roof of Greenland. It is also the habitat of Greenland's most interesting fauna. Anaq and I studied gyrfalcons on Clavering Island, counted musk oxen around King Oscar's Fjord, and tracked the last surviving polar wolf in Peary Land.

"One day, an American Air Force captain carrying a briefcase came to see me here in Tasiilaq; at that time the Yanks still had a radar installation on Kulusuk Island. He asked if he could talk to me in confidence. I shut the door to my office, and he pulled out a large file of aerial photographs. Some had been taken from B-17s flying across the southern third of Greenland during the Second World War. Others were more recent and far more detailed—god knows what kind of American spy plane might have taken them.

"But the point is that all these photographs were of that relatively unknown segment of the southeast coast around Puisortoq." Dansgaard glanced at Qav, who was shuddering at hearing the-name-that-could-not-be-spoken.

"Yes, Puisortoq, feared not just by the Inuit, but by anyone who has ever had the misfortune to travel that hellish coastline." Dansgaard's face darkened. "I'm sure Qav or his grandfather has told you that my beloved wife died there. She perished because of my stupidity or rather, my arrogant disregard for the wisdom of the Greenlanders."

He stopped for a moment, seemingly at the point of tears, then gathered his composure.

"I'm sorry. At any event, my tragedy was still in the future. At that time I was young and sure of myself. Anaq and I had conquered the most dangerous terrains in Greenland, including the Inland Ice and the remote Northeast Foreland. So when the American captain showed me his extraordinary photographs, I was overwhelmed by excitement, by the lust of discovery."

"Tell us about the photographs," begged Julia. The kids leaned forward in their seats.

"The American didn't know how to interpret them. The photos showed a labyrinth of deep, fjord-like valleys just south of Puisortoq and north of Igutsaat Fjord. They were unusual, to say the least, because they were not incised down to sea level as is typical for glacial-carved valleys. Instead, they were hanging valleys ending in high cliffs above the ocean, thus invisible from the sea. Undoubtedly Nansen and others had passed by, probably admiring the high waterfalls, or in winter, icefalls, but without a clue as to their source.

"But if they were geologically unusual, this was nothing compared to their astounding vegetation. They were even greener and more thickly forested with willow than the most temperate areas of southwestern Greenland, where the Vikings had settled with their cattle and sheep. This, of course, is very strange, so close to Puisortoq and the Inland Ice. This is what the American captain wanted me to explain.

"My hunch—which I didn't disclose to the American—was that this richness of vegetation was due to thermal springs, possibly even geysers. It appeared to be an extraordinary oasis, a possible refugia for near-extinct plants and wildlife."

Conor turned to look at Jack, who had become visibly nervous and was squirming around in his seat. "Why is this upsetting him?" Conor wondered. Then suddenly he remembered Jack's dream: each detail matched Dansgaard's description. He would have to tell Qav about it later.

"The American made a proposal. He was curious about the region but was unprepared to mount an expensive expedition. He had heard about our adventures—Anaq and I traveled cheap—and he told me that his government would finance my little research station for a year if we would explore the mystery valleys south of Puisortoq.

"Truth was, I was so excited by the photographs that Anaq and I would have been off in a few days anyway, but I told him I would weigh the proposition, discuss it with local officials, and get back to him in a few days. The very next day, of course, Anaq and I were packing our gear.

"There is obviously no safe way to traverse Puisortoq, although in the winter it's less dangerous. But I didn't want to wait that long. Also, if there was wildlife—say, reindeer—it would be much easier to find and document them in the summer. So we sent a message to the American and arranged for a local fisherman to take us and our kayaks as far south as he could be bribed to go. In effect, this was to Cape Bille, the northern edge of Puisortoq. My wife was keen to accompany us, but I insisted that she stay home, this time, at least."

Dansgaard stopped for a minute. He tapped the ash out of his pipe and refilled it with fresh tobacco. Qav fetched a bowl of water for Anori. Julia absentmindedly fiddled with her bear amulet. Conor shot a look at Jack, who seemed calmer. Then Dansgaard resumed.

"Puisortoq was, as I should've known, a sheer nightmare. Qav, your grandfather was never braver, especially in the face of his certain conviction that we would be killed. The ice face is five hundred feet high, perhaps higher. Not only does it calve icebergs from its towering face, but even more notoriously, from its submerged base. Many travelers have been killed by the unexpected eruption of a giant berg out of the sea in front of them." Dansgaard tapped his pipe on his palm for emphasis.

"That day there was a thick fog, and we had to tie a rope between our kayaks to keep from losing each other. It was eerier than you can possibly imagine: utter silence punctuated by strange keening noises and sharp-pitched cries. That's why it is called—at least for those who even speak its name—'the place of screaming ice.'

"Scientifically, of course, we can attribute these sounds to the terrific pressures inside the ice sheet as it fissures, cracks, and breaks apart. But that doesn't diminish the terror. Especially when you know that at any moment—it happens, on average, once an hour—an enormous splinter of the ice sheet, perhaps as tall as a twenty-story building, could tumble on top of you. Or worse, slide under the water and then explode from beneath your kayak, hurtling you a hundred feet in the air. Being in the fog only made the tension more unbearable.

"We had paddled for more than three hours—remember what I just said about the average hourly interval between ice calvings—when in back of us we heard a sound like no other in the world. A huge minaret of ice had torn away from the very top of the ice sheet and was falling—so we thought—on top of us. In fact, it was more than a mile, maybe even two miles, to our rear. But the wave it produced was nearly twenty-five feet high.

"Do any of you surf?"

Julia nodded yes, while the other three shook their heads.

"Well, Anaq and I certainly had never had the experience until the giant wave picked up our tiny kayaks and rocketed us forward. We frantically struggled to keep upright, unsure whether we were being propelled out to sea or into the side of an iceberg or cliff.

"We thought, of course, that we were doomed. But the tidal wave hurled us through the fog into sudden bright sunshine. The wave slowly flattened into a gentle swell. All around us were bobbing corklike fragments of shattered glacial ice and menacing growlers—small icebergs. But our kayaks were still intact, and in front of us was a narrow shelf of rock, the foot of an almost vertical cliff of two-billion-year-old Greenland gneiss. Spilling over the top was a large stream, the waterfall was perhaps two hundred feet high. At its base, the pressure of the falling water had blasted a crater into the shelf rock, where it mixed with the pounding sea.

"It was a sublime sight, and I knew instantly that we were below the first of the valleys in the American aerial photographs. But how to reach the top? Anaq pointed to a jagged diagonal crack in the rock that started to the left of the waterfall, passed behind it, and emerged to the right of it. Toward the top of the cliff it widened into what Alpinists call a 'couloir,' a steep rock-filled gully.

"It was a tricky, even hair-raising climb that took most of the day, but to be honest, we were more concerned about where we could safely leave our kayaks: the sea shelf was too narrow and probably lashed by high tide. We eventually had to wedge both kayaks in the bottom twenty feet of the crack and hope that they would not be crushed by falling rocks or debris.

"Anaq, as usual, despite being nine years older than me, was first to the top. But he said nothing. 'Anaq,' I yelled, 'what do you see?' Again no reply. I was annoyed, and I shimmied up the couloir, wrestling with loose rocks. Finally I pulled myself over the last boulder. Anaq was on his knees, staring straight ahead and mumbling some ancient incantation, a shamanic poem.

"I started to reproach him when I too was struck speechless. The valley in front of us was perhaps three or four miles wide, with steep crenellated granite sides rising four or five hundred feet high. It extended inland perhaps eight or nine miles until another ridge neatly divided it into a 'Y.' The two smaller, tributary valleys climbed two or three miles to icefields or small hanging glaciers.

"But what took our speech away was its greenness. It looked like a mountain valley in the Alps or in southern Norway, nothing like anyone in East Greenland had ever seen or even imagined. And staggeringly, straight in front of us, on a mound twenty or thirty feet above the stream, was a ruined stone-and-turf structure, a large house or perhaps a small citadel."

Dansgaard stopped and smiled. He laid his pipe in an ashtray and walked across the room to a small safe. He turned the dial once to the right, then to the left, then twice around to the right again. He shuffled around inside the safe for a minute, then found a thin folder. He passed it around to the kids.

19. VALLEY OF THE RUNES

Inside the folder were half a dozen photographs. Although they were black and white, the lushness of the valley was nonetheless apparent. There were carpets of flowers and dense willow groves near the stream. And incredibly, there was the ruin: it had a massive stone foundation with walls of smaller boulders infilled with cobble. It had three narrow, slotlike windows with outside ledges and a small arched door. Most of the turf roof was collapsed, but an impressive stone chimney was largely intact.

"Doctor, this isn't an Inuit home," exclaimed Qav.

"No, obviously not," laughed Dansgaard. "Well, kids, what do you make of these photos? Anaq and I took them on our trip."

"European," said Julia, "the kind of structure that a party of explorers, or possibly downed airmen, might build if they knew they would have to winter over. It is, however, unusually massive."

"Good guess, Julia," said Dansgaard. "Jack, Conor, what do you think?"

"Julia is right." Jack had been reading about polar exploration since he was seven. He knew that the secret of survival in the Arctic was economy of effort. "No one overwintering would expend so much unnecessary labor. It doesn't make sense."

"Unless," Conor added, "they were actually constructing a permanent home, or a position to defend against some enemy."

"It looks like Bishop's house in Igaliku," suggested Qav with some amazement.

"Yes, you are all correct. It is far too massive to be a temporary dwelling. And it does look like the famous house in Igaliku, or as the Norse called it, Gardar, in southwest Greenland, which was built by Bishop Arnald in 1124."

Everyone was now wide-eyed.

Dansgaard went back to the safe and returned with one more photograph. He passed it around. "Wow," said Conor and Jack, while Julia and Qav were less sure what they were looking at.

"Some kind of hieroglyphics?" Julia said tentatively.

"Actually, they're runes," said Jack, "a stone carved with the enigmatic symbols of the Viking rune language."

"There's a good collection of them in the National Museum in Dublin," added Conor.

"Oh, yeah," Qav now remembered, "there are rune stones in our national museum as well, in Nuuk."

Dansgaard was pleased. "Yes, runes. This is a Norse house. Imagine how astonished Anaq and I were to discover a Viking ruin—the Vikings never colonized East Greenland, or at least that was the accepted wisdom until we climbed into this unexplored valley."

"But I thought the Danes, Lieutenant Holm and all, came to the east coast in the 1880s because they thought that the Vikings might have survived here," Julia said.

"Yes, that's true. For hundreds of years Norwegians, Danes, and others believed that the lost 'East Colony' of Viking Greenland might be where Tasiilaq is. Holm indeed convinced himself that the locals were the offspring of Norse and Inuit.[8] But it was simply a mistake. The 'East Colony' is actually on the west coast, south of the 'West Colony.'"

"That is confusing." Conor shook his head.

"We believed that we had found evidence of a *third* colony, unknown from the Icelandic sagas or the Greenland archive in Bergen—maybe the last holdout of the Norse, who perhaps had been shipwrecked or for some reason went into hiding."

"That's incredible," said Jack, somewhat relieved that a crucial detail of Dansgaard's story was unlike his dream. "But what do the runes say?"

Dansgaard pushed his spectacles further up his nose and stared intensely at Jack. "They say, as best I can decipher them: 'God save us from Satan, straelings, and witches.' 'Straelings,' of course, was the derogatory Norse word for the Inuit."

"What a spooky message," Jack whispered to himself. Conor shuddered in solidarity. Qav looked apprehensively at his friends.

"But how about the bones?" Julia demanded, in her slightly brassy New York accent. She was unimpressed by the diabolic implication. "Did you see mammoths on this trip?"

Dansgaard chuckled. "I told you this was a long story. On this first trip we saw no evidence of mammoths. Nor had that fantastic possibility entered our heads. Surprisingly, we saw no wildlife at all, which was puzzling to me. We were anxious to go back. We didn't have the proper equipment for a full reconnaissance. I wanted to go back to Tasiilaq, develop the photos, and then come back to stay the entire winter. After all, we had a splendid bivouac in the great Norse house."

Anori yawned.

"I know tonight has been both exciting and confusing, so I will end this part of my saga now. You need time to reflect on what you have seen and heard. We will meet in exactly one week. Then I will relate Part Two, the infinitely sadder second half of my tale. You will learn everything that I now know, including the story of the mammoth bones. To bed, my young friends."

Frankly, the gang would have stayed up for a week to hear every detail of this extraordinary tale, but they recognized how painful it was for Dansgaard to recall the details of the tragic second expedition. So they anxiously counted days until the following Sunday.

EPISODE FOUR: *A New Expedition*

*T*he kids' curiosity would have killed a thousand cats, so they kept busy as best they could. Jack fiddled with his trike, increasingly frustrated that he would never have the opportunity to fly it himself. Julia, meanwhile, had covered an entire wall with reindeer photographs and seemed determined to give each a name and personality.

Qav and Conor had a better distraction: they went kayaking. Conor was an experienced kayaker (his second favorite sport after mountaineering), but a few minutes paddling with Qav demonstrated how much he still had to learn. Although Qav's friends sometimes taunted him as *"tikeraaq"*—"the tourist"—because he was now boarding most of the year in Copenhagen, he was the finest kayaker his age on the east coast. Having been taught by his grandfather from a very young age, he glided across the water effortlessly, making it impossible for Conor, or anyone, to catch him.

"Come on, Conor, let me show you the Inuit way to paddle. You are working too hard. Hold the paddle lower with the blade tilted forward thirty degrees. Now rotate your torso with each stroke. . . . That's right. Let the more powerful muscles of your back do the work, not your arms. Focus on the end of your stroke and steadily increase the cadence."[9]

Conor carefully followed Qav's instructions, and the improvement in his paddling efficiency was dramatic. They smiled at each other. Now this was the real thing: racing across the quicksilver surface of the fjord, dodging icebergs while pretending to stalk seals and polar bears.

After an hour or so, they stopped for lunch on the far shore of King Oscar's Havn—the arm of Ammassalik Fjord on which Tasiilaq is sited. Towering above them was a stunning two-thousand-meter peak that was a favorite climb for visiting mountaineers.

"Did you know that the Greenland Vikings were part-Irish?"

Conor laughed. "Come on, Qav, you're pulling my leg for sure."

"No, I am serious. The early settlers that Erik the Red brought from Iceland in 985 were about 40 percent Irish. Vilhjalmur Stefansson, the great Arctic explorer, devoted a whole section in his book on Greenland to the Irish slaves and bondsmen who came with the Vikings."[10]

"No leprechauns?"

Now Qav laughed.

"Listen, Qav, I hate to change the subject, but there is something I have to tell you." Conor was suddenly serious. He related the story of Jack's dream and the similarities to Dansgaard's description of the mystery valley.

Qav listened quietly. He didn't seem surprised by the strange coincidence.

"This may be far-fetched, but is it possible that someone sent Jack that dream, just like your grandfather sends dreams to you in Denmark?" asked Conor.

"Yeah, I was thinking the same thing."

"Your grandfather?"

"Perhaps, or someone else."

"Like who? Come on now, you don't mean *his* grandfather, the ancient sorcerer, do you?"

Qav chuckled. "Well, let's leave that aside for the moment. I was really thinking of Dansgaard. The old Viking knows almost as much of our pre-Christian culture as my grandfather. Perhaps he has achieved the power to send dreams."

"Hmm. That would explain a lot." Conor told Qav about the strange questions that Dansgaard had sent to Jack.

"'Where are the mammoths?,' indeed! I'm going to die of terminal frustration if I can't see those mammoths with my own eyes."

"You are not suggesting that we go there, are you?" Qav had a sly expression.

"Well, Qav, you are the best kayaker on the coast and I'm the mammoth geek."

"What would Jack say?"

"He'd kill me. Not a chance he'd let me go."

"Nor my parents either. My mother already thinks my grandfather has too much superstitious influence on me—that's probably the real reason they sent me to school in Denmark."

"So we're bolloxed."

"Bolloxed?"

"Sorry, your English is so good, I forgot you don't know Dublinese.

I mean we can't go, but then again, we'll die of curiosity if we don't go."

"I know, Conor, as much as Puisortoq scares me, what an incredible adventure it would be. The chance to become a famous Inuit hero like my grandad. And for you, a real mammoth, maybe."

"Look, let's play a little game. We know we can't go, but let's just pretend that we are going anyway and figure out a strategy. Let's organize an imaginary expedition. At least we'll feel less frustrated and useless."

"Hey, that's a great idea. Let's go back to Tasiilaq and see what kind of gear we can find—for our purely imaginary adventure, I mean."

Both laughed and paddled back.

21. A FANTASY FLIGHT

Jack was in the Institute's workroom, tinkering with an autopilot system for the Icehawk. The trike had been designed for him to fly, so it had been delicately calibrated to respond not just to his hand controls but also to subtle shifts in the weight of his body. It was more like an aerial skateboard than an ordinary flying machine. Now getting the remote controls to work was damnably difficult.

Jack was so absorbed in his frustrating work that he didn't notice Julia, who had been watching silently for almost ten minutes.

"It's beautiful," said Julia.

"Hiya," said Jack, looking up with a socket wrench in his hand.

"So who invented the first trike?" Julia was now at Jack's side.

"Hard to say, actually, one ancestor was the *Bachstelze*, a tiny, rotor-driven glider that German U-boats during the Second World War towed behind them as an observation platform. When a destroyer was spotted, the submarine crash-dived, and the unlucky pilot usually drowned."

"And how is a trike different from a hang glider?"

"Well, it can be used as a hang glider, but with its two power sources—the solar cells and hydrogen batteries—it can also fly for hours and at fairly high altitudes. I designed it to be the workhorse for small scientific expeditions. It provides air reconnaissance capability with little more additional weight or bulk than a canoe."

"Travel light, travel smart, eh?"

"Sure, that's the mantra of today's bold young explorers." Jack smiled.

"It's beautiful, but it looks too delicate to support anyone's weight."

"There are actually two seats. I designed it to carry Conor and me as well as a small instrument package. The structural components are incredibly strong."

"Well, you're lucky you won't be risking your life in any test flights."

"No, I don't suppose I will," said Jack, bitterly.

"Don't look so grim, Jack." Julia tried to console him.

"Well, I've worked on this since I was twelve, with one dream: to fly it myself. Now Dansgaard insists that I have to convert it into a big remoted-controlled toy. For what purpose?"

Julia became more serious. "I don't think he really wants to count reindeer. After all, we could simply ask Qav's grandfather if that's all we wanted to know."

"Of course. I think Dansgaard means to track mammoths with it. I think he wants me to send it to the mystery valley."

"Will it work?"

"I'm not sure, Julia. If I flew it, yes, it would work. But as a drone, I'm not optimistic. It's like trying to surf or ski by remote control."

"Would it support both of our weights?"

Jack sized Julia up carefully. "Probably. Do you want to fly away with me to the land of lost mammoths?" Jack was half-serious.

Julia laughed. "Well, I can fantasize, can't I?"

22. DANSGAARD'S TALE (PART TWO)

Sunday night finally came. The team gathered in the Institute at ten. Dansgaard seemed quite nervous as he paced back and forth. The dog, Anori, sensed his state and moved away.

"I told you before that Anaq and I returned to Tasiilaq with one thought: to quickly return to the valley for the entire winter. We planned to load a motorboat with food, heating oil, hunting rifles, and other supplies. We figured we could build a new turf roof for the Norse house and settle in snugly until we could explore the valley by skis. We'd tell no one about our discovery until we had returned again with film, maps, archaelogical evidence.

"But of course, I did tell one other person." Dansgaard was now talking to himself or, rather, to a ghost.

"I told my young wife, Tusu. She was beautiful, fearless, and an excellent outdoorswoman. Although she was a true Greenlander, she had been educated in Denmark. She no longer embraced the old beliefs or superstitions—even dreaded Puisortoq failed to frighten her. She was determined to accompany us.

"What happened is too painful for me to relate in any detail. Suffice it to say that Anaq, Tusu, and I left a week later. Our powerful motorboat, loaded with a winter's worth of supplies, pulled our kayaks in tow. The weather was unusually calm and bright, with broad channels of blue water between the icebergs. When we arrived just north of Puisortoq, we camped, waiting for the perfect moment to tempt fate."

Dansgaard was silent for a moment or two. "We started the treacherous passage in fine weather. Puisortoq was again eerily silent. We had been out for about two hours and were two-thirds of the way across the mouth of the ice sheet. Suddenly there was a high-pitched wail, truly indescribable. Then the world went black. Anaq pulled me from the water unconscious. He had saved my life. We never found Tusu's body.

"In the face of this hideous tragedy, which I knew Anaq believed we had provoked by our defiance of Puisortoq and its demons, we abandoned any plan, indeed any interest in the lost Viking colony. I went back to Denmark for almost a year. When I returned the following summer—still grieving for my young wife—Anaq and I resumed our explorations in the north. We did not speak about the Valley of the Runes again for years.

"But a few years ago I began to have nightly dreams—incessant dreams—of the valley, where I saw my dead wife, alive in a meadow. The dreams were like a narcotic. I could hardly bear being awake, when every night I could return to my wife.

"Anaq, of course, believed the dreams were more than the nostalgia of an old man. He insisted that someone—certainly not him—had sent the dreams. But who? I no longer completely discounted such a possibility. The more I thought about it, and the more I dreamed, the more convinced I was that my wife was still alive in some Greenlandic Shangri-la."

The kids were becoming uneasy.

"In the end I had to return to that place, and Anaq came with me. Going in the winter by dogsled reduced the danger of Puisortoq, but we had enormous difficulty ascending the cliff face. We were both older, and I, at least was weaker, plus the great crack was now coated with slick ice. It took us two days to bolt ropes and aluminum ladders to the cliff—where, by the way, they remain."

"Your wife?" Poor Qav was wide-eyed.

"No, Qav," Dansgaard's expression was now gentle. "My young wife did not run into my arms. My dream wasn't real. But stranger things did occur."

The kids' anxiety was almost electric.

"First, someone had rebuilt the roof of the Viking house. Not recently, but certainly since we had last visited so many years before. And secondly, we found a pile of bones outside the house. Mammoth bones. I assumed, of course, that they were thousands of years old, but they seemed to be in an extraordinary state of preservation, as if the great beast had died only a few weeks before.

"We stayed but one night. Our nervous dogs were tethered to sleds at the bottom of the cliff, and we could hear them howling in terror. I didn't really sleep—afraid, I suppose, of what I might dream. The next morning, which of course was only a vague twilight, we lowered ourselves and a few of the bones back down the cliff. Our dogs looked crazed, as if they spend the night with ghosts. Several had managed to bite through their thick leather leads and had disappeared.

"Anaq and I spent several hours looking for our lost dogs, but we didn't find them. Just as we were giving up the search, Anori emerged out of the mist: a great elkhound like those the Vikings took with them to Greenland to hunt reindeer. He simply trotted up to us and never left our side.

"The trip back to Tasiilaq was uneventful, yet a strange tension, almost a madness, persisted amongst the dogs, who refused to go near Anori. After our arrival, Anaq immediately returned to his home, while I began to examine and test the mammoth bones.

"I thought I'd gone mad, just like my sled dogs. Under the microscope I saw the cellular tissue of fresh death. My carbon-14 tests gave utterly impossible results. Week after week I repeated the same tests and obtained the same results. I sent for mammoth and mastodon bone samples from Canada, Sweden, and Siberia. My equipment was working perfectly. Gradually I had to accept the stupendous conclusion: mammoths still existed.

"Now I conceived a plan. UNESCO had been after me for several years to host a summer school in Tasiilaq. Yes, I told them, send me four outstanding young scientists.

"I did my own research. Qav, of course, was the pride of East Greenland, so he was the first chosen. Jack I knew about from news stories about his ingenious trike. Of course, you can't imagine how astounded I was to discover that his younger brother had won top prize in the Dublin Science Fair with his project on ancient mammoths in Britain. This left only one slot. I needed an extraordinarily competent mammalian biologist. After reading about Julia's research in Spitzbergen, she was the obvious choice. A perfect team."

"But why kids?" asked Jack. "Why didn't you go straight to senior scientists, your colleagues? You would've immediately had immense financial support, been able to mount a huge expedition, have your picture on the cover of every news magazine in the world . . . "

Dansgaard interrupted him. "That's precisely why I chose you. I want no publicity whatsoever. Do you realize what a media land rush would do to mammoth ecology, to East Greenland? No, the last thing I wanted was some corporate nightmare of Pleistocene Park and a million tourists with their cameras descending on the last viable hunting communities in the Arctic."

"But aren't you afraid that we'll tell? How can you trust us?" asked Julia provocatively.

"Simple," said Dansgaard. "You're kids. Who would believe you, or take your word against mine about something so fantastic as living mammoths? The world would laugh out loud, and you, my dear friends, would suddenly find it very difficult to get into the universities of your choice."

"That's diabolical," responded Julia in anger.

"No . . . actually I think it's quite clever," said Conor, to everyone else's surprise. "Dr. Dansgaard is quite right. The world—or rather the corporate media—really couldn't handle a discovery like this. They would unleash a tidal wave of commercialism, tourism, and publicity. It would destroy the culture of Greenland."

Qav smiled at Conor, proud that his friend understood the stakes.

"Hmmm . . . I think I see your point," said Julia, reflecting on what disasters even minor bear-watching tourism had brought to her favorite Arctic carnivores in Alaska and Canada.

Dansgaard was beaming. "Excellent. I knew you could be trusted. You were selected not just for your precocious knowledge, but because each of you had a special sensitivity to wild creation."

"OK, Doc," said Jack. "You've told us your secrets, and we, in turn, have passed your tests of intuition and discretion. What's next? What is the plan?"

23. THE BIRD PEOPLE

"Do you know where Tingmiarmiut is?" asked Dansgaard.

"It's an abandoned Inuit village about 180 miles south of here, near Mogens Heinesen Fjord," replied Jack, who had obviously done his geography homework.

"Yes, it is only about a few miles north of . . . ," Qav hesitated before the dreaded word. ". . . of Puisortoq. The name means 'bird people,' because my ancestors often hunted birds—terns, ptarmigans, and kittiwakes—there in the late summer. But it has a bad reputation."

"What do you mean?" asked Julia.

"Well, in the fall and winter it is often blasted by the Piteraq, the icy hurricane that blows off the Inland Ice. Also, people didn't like being so near to . . . Puisortoq. No one has lived there for generations, although it is sometimes visited by hunters."

"And now by you," added Dansgaard. "Tingmiarmiut will be base camp for the five of us, plus Qav's grandfather. We'll take a small fishing boat loaded with a month's supplies, plus kayaks and Jack's trike. As far as anyone else is concerned, we are going to Tingmiarmiut to study summer bird life. Can I count on you keeping our real mission a secret?"

The gang looked at each other. "Of course, Dr. Dansgaard," replied Julia for all of them.

Dansgaard was pleased. "The four of you will set up and man our communications station. It consists of a shortwave radio, a Global Positioning Satellite locator and this . . ." He motioned to the corner of the museum. "That's a video transmission system. The images picked up in the field by handheld cameras will be relayed to the remote-controlled trike in flight, then beamed back to you in Tingmiarmiut."

"Wait a second, Dr. Dansgaard." Conor looked concerned. "What do you mean 'back to us?' Where will you and Anaq be?"

Dansgaard looked very grave. "Anaq and I are returning by kayaks to the Valley of the Runes. We will keep in constant contact with you by radio. If we locate the mammoths, you will launch the trike, keeping it high enough above the Inland Ice so that we can transmit the images back to you."

"Wait, wait," said Jack. "After all you have told us about the dangers of Puisortoq, why are you going by kayak? Surely we could arrange for one of the local helicopters to ferry us to the valley. It would be infinitely safer, and we could all go."

"No, Jack, I'm afraid that is impossible," said Dansgaard. "The valley is beyond the fuel range of a helicopter."

"Well, we could ferry aviation fuel to Tingmiarmiut by boat, then clear a helicopter pad, and . . ."

Dansgaard again interrupted Jack. "No, we can't do that. The pilot would have to obtain permission from local authorities. They, in turn, would demand specific details of our expedition. Its secrecy would be compromised, and we would become laughingstocks or worse."

"But Dr. Dansgaard, take us with you," Conor implored.

"Of course not. Under no circumstances. I would never put your lives in jeopardy."

"But how about yours?" replied Julia.

Dansgaard chuckled. "Anaq and I are very old men. If Puisortoq decides to devour us, it would be a fitting end to two lifetimes of adventure. We are quite reconciled to the dangers. You see, my children, we have thought this through in every detail."

"But what," asked Qav somewhat desperately, "is the point of all this, if we can't disclose any of our findings to the world?"

"As scientists," said Dansgaard solemnly, "we have a responsibility to resolve this mystery and to understand the ecology of the mammoths' survival in this extraordinary refugia. When we know more about the environment, the numbers and health of the creatures themselves, then we can begin to discuss a plan for gradually revealing their existence, first to other scientists, then perhaps to the world. But until we know more, we have must preserve secrecy at all costs."

The kids were very unhappy with the prospect of Dansgaard and Anaq again tempting Puisortoq, but Dansgaard's strategy had an irresistible logic that none of them could easily refute.

"OK, Professor," said Jack. "I can see how carefully you have planned all of this. But I'm not sure that I guarantee that the trike can successfully fulfill its part of the mission without the hand of a pilot."

"Jack, please hear this clearly," replied Dansgaard. "If you can't operate the Icehawk from the ground, so be it. We will make a video log and bring it back with us. But under no circumstances—and I mean absolutely NO circumstances—are you to attempt to fly it yourself. Understood?"

Julia glanced sideways at Jack. He looked downcast. "Yes, I promise," conceded Jack reluctantly.

"Well, good," Dansgaard was cheerful again. "We have three days to pack all of our gear. Julia, please help Jack with the Icehawk. When you are finished with that, you can start familiarizing yourself with the radio equipment. I will manage with the rest of the gear, while Qav and Conor take charge of our fishing boat. Anaq arrives tomorrow. Any other questions?"

Everyone had brightened up at the prospect of adventure, even Jack.

"OK, gang," Dansgaard sounded positively youthful. "We're off to the place of the bird people."

EPISODE FIVE: *Everyone Disappears!*

*I*t took two days to outfit the expedition. Tasiilaq is a small town, so there was considerable curiosity about the departure of Dr. Dansgaard's summer school. A group of Qav's friends gathered around the small fishing boat that had been rented for the two-week trip to Tingmiarmiut.

Several of the kids were particularly intrigued by the odd-looking electronic apparatus that Conor was carefully packing into a crate.

"What's that?" one of them asked Conor in Greenlandic. "It looks like a very funny radio." Qav translated.

Conor surprised Qav by blushing. "Oh . . . it's a . . . well, it's . . . you know . . ." he stuttered uncharacteristically. Then he recovered. "It picks up and magnifies faint animal sounds. Like birds."

It took awhile for Qav to translate the idea. The kids chuckled, then moved on to help Jack and Julia stow the Icehawk and the six kayaks that the expedition was taking.

Qav took Conor aside. "OK, what is that device? What does it really do?"

Conor answered with a devilish grin. "As I said, it amplifies faint sounds. In fact, it's tuned to frequencies totally inaudible to the human ear."

Qav was puzzled. "You mean like the sounds made by dolphins and whales?"

"Exactly, except these sounds are made by elephants and mammoths."

"But I thought elephants . . . trumpeted?" Qav was embarrassed that he had only seen a real elephant once, in the Copenhagen Zoo.

"Oh, they make a wide range of sounds that we hear variously as growls, rumbles, trumpets, or screams. But they converse with themselves at low frequencies we can't distinguish."

"They do?" Qav was fascinated that the huge beasts had their own secret language.

"Yes, but scientists only found this out recently. In 1987 researchers discovered that Indian elephants can communicate over amazing distances using infrasonic signals, below the threshold of human hearing.

This solved the old mystery of how widely separated herds—kilometers apart—could move cross-country in perfect coordination."[11]

"So you think mammoths and mastodons had the same ability?"

"Almost certainly," replied Conor. "This apparatus—which I made for the Dublin Science Fair—can pick up infrasounds at a range of ten, maybe even twenty kilometers. Its directional rangefinder will allow us to pinpoint the mammoths long before we actually see them."

"You said 'us.'" Qav gave Conor a long look. "But we are under strict orders to stay at the base camp."

"Of course, me boy," said Conor. "But you never know what may happen on an expedition."

Qav thought hard for a moment and then grinned. "Well, we do have our kayaks on board, and enough gear to survive a few weeks by ourselves if we had to . . ." Now Qav was playing the devil.

Conor laughed, then became serious again. "Remember, Qav, not a word to my brother about our plan. OK?"

"Hunter's honor. But on your side, not a word to my grandfather. He would skin me alive or turn me into a *tupilak*."

The two friends shook hands.

25. THE DEPARTURE

It had been the expedition's intention to slip away quietly. But Qav's parents, his friends, and indeed, most of Tasiilaq turned out to wave and cheer good-bye from the promontory above the boat inlet. Dansgaard's little vessel, with its sputtering diesel engine, chugged out bravely into the fjord, dodging a few elderly icebergs. On the left was the magnificent Matterhorn-like peak with an unpronounceable name: Qimmeertaajaliip Qaqqartivaa.

It took only twenty minutes to reach the open sea. With the power-ful East Greenland Current pushing it from behind, the little boat's engine no longer had to strain. The expedition was suddenly gliding southward at full speed. The sky over the coast was clear, but to the east, giant cotton-candy cumulus clouds grew as high as the stratosphere.

Jack imagined what their expedition would look like from the window of the one of the transatlantic passenger jets whose contrails so often streaked the sky above Tasiilaq: just a tiny red dot amidst the endless procession of icebergs headed south to menace the shipping lanes of Newfoundland. "The iceberg that sank the *Titanic* passed this way once," he thought to himself.

After an hour they had passed Cape Tycho Brahe, the mouth of the great Sermilik Fjord on the back side of Ammassalik Island. Qav and Conor were at the wheel, intensely concentrated on maneuvering the boat between icebergs, some of which were now as big as small mountains. They were benevolently watched over by Dansgaard, who was smoking his beautiful old-fashioned pipe carved from walrus ivory in the shape of a mermaid. Julia was with the great dog Anori in the bow; both were exhilarated by the cold wind and bright sunlight on their faces.

Jack, inside the cabin with Anaq, was showing the ancient hunter how to work the powerful video recorder that also acted as a GPS locator and cellular radio. Anaq was fascinated by Europeans' wonderful toys, although he preferred the old-fashioned Inuit computer in his own head with its extraordinary stored memory of places and routes.

Jack's Greenlandic had made remarkable progress in the last month, but he still felt like an infant trying to speak for the first time. He formulated his words as carefully as possible. "I'm worried about Conor and Qav," he said quietly.

Anaq gently nodded. He replied as simply as he could. "The boys are too brave. They do not yet understand danger."

"I worry that . . ." Jack was groping for the right words. "I worry that they may go to the place of the . . ." He didn't have a clue how to say the "place of the mammoths." He tried another tack. "I worry that they may follow you."

Anaq gave a long wise look. "Yes, I worry too. But you must make them stay at base, stay with you—do you understand, Jack?"

Jack nodded. "Yes, Anaq, of course." But he thought to himself: "Keeping Conor from his mammoths: That will be a challenge!"

A little after 2 A.M., dusk just below the Arctic Circle, they stopped the little boat's engine and anchored in a calm, ice-free inlet for six hours of sleep. They awoke at 8 A.M. to see Anaq returning in his kayak with some berries he picked ashore. "The fishing is lousy," he told Dansgaard, "but here is a trout and a bucket of bilberries for the children's breakfast."

Conor and Qav, the two young sailors, again took the wheel while Dansgaard made breakfast below. It was Anaq's turn to light a pipe while Anori curled at his feet. It was a beautiful day, brisk and bright. They passed an iceberg shaped uncannily like an ancient Spanish galleon. The ice at its waterline was a startling turquoise.

"Where are we?" Julia asked. Jack translated the question to Anaq.

"Igtip Kangertiva," Anaq pronounced the name very slowly. "The war camp of the Americans."

Jack's eyes lit up. "Oh, Comanche Bay." He explained to Julia that the Yanks had built a weather station and rescue base here during the Second World War after a flight of B-17s had crashed on the Inland Ice.

The coast was magnificent, reminiscent of Alaska or Norway, but also sad and haunted. Qav told his friends a tragic story.

At one time several hundred Inuit, keepers of the ancient East Greenlandic culture, wintered in the inlets between Puisortoq and Tasiilaq, but in the nineteenth century the climate changed and the seals came less frequently to the fjords of the southeastern coast. Hunters wandered dangerously far out onto the field ice, but no seals could be found. As hunger turned their children into skeletons, desperate mothers gathered lichen or dug up their own garbage.

Some blamed the famine on the Ingnerajuaitsiat, evil dwarfs who live in caves in the Inland Ice, or the Erqigdlit, men with the heads of dogs. Still others accused their own shamans, the *angakoq*, like Anaq's grandfather. A frenzy of murder and revenge engulfed the lonely households.

In the end, a few families survived by practicing cannibalism, while more withered and died in their winter homes. By the time Holm arrived in Tasiilaq looking for lost Vikings in 1884, only about four hundred hungry people survived. Except for the district around Ammassalik and Sermilik Fjords, the rest of the east coast was a graveyard.

Now, as their little red boat chugged south, Qav and his grandfather pointed out the occasional rock ruins and turf mounds—the "dead houses"—where their ancestors had starved and perished. Qav told them that in the early 1930s the great Knud Rasmussen had counted no fewer than 158 abandoned houses along that stretch of the south-eastern coast still known as "The Dead Land."

Anaq began to softly chant an old song:

> *Towards the south, I could see*
> *The hazy mountains,*
> *Where all our kinfolk live,*
> *All those who are dear to us . . .*
>
> *On those shores live our mothers,*
> *Down there lived our aunts . . . our uncles . . .*
> *Down there in the South*
> *Lived all our beloved relations . . .*

Conor and Jack recalled what they had learned in school about Ireland's Great Hunger in the 1840s when one million people had starved. Yet, relative to population, the famine described by Qav killed far more, perhaps fully 60 percent of the East Greenland people. It was a tragedy of almost incomprehensible magnitude.[12]

Qav explained that because of the famine, most of the East Greenlanders didn't resist the establishment of a Danish trading station or the coming of missionaries. His grandfather's grandfather, of course, was an exception: he had disappeared somewhere in the south rather than live under European beliefs.

Conor asked Qav about Greenland today. "My family supports Inuit Ataqatigitt—the Human Brotherhood Party—which wants a union of all the Inuit people in the Arctic. As a start, we want a fully independent Greenland. And we want the United States to dismantle their huge nuclear airbase in Thule, in northwest Greenland."

Qav looked anxiously at Julia. "I hope you don't think I'm anti-American."

Julia laughed. "Of course not, Qav. I agree with you. This is your land . . . and the polar bears'."

At midnight the expedition cast its anchor near the cliffs of Umanaq, an area renowned for its berries, sorrel and angelica. They had heard that a family still lived here, but their bright blue house—the last vestige of habitation this far south—was boarded up. Anaq guessed that they were either in Tasiilaq, or as some modern Greenlanders prefer, in Spain on their summer holiday!

27. BASE CAMP

They shoved off early the next morning, and within a few hours the spectacular pinnacles of Tingmiarmiut came into view. The horizon was a saw blade of sharp peaks with hanging ice fields and small valley glaciers. Offshore were a number of small flat islands, their surfaces polished by an ancient ice sheet. These islands were much favored by seabirds.

Anaq took the wheel from Conor and expertly maneuvered between the rocks and shards of icebergs. They tied up to a tiny quay. Overhead a migrant raven cawed what could be interpreted as either a welcome or a warning.

Tingmiarmiut consisted of the ruins of half a dozen old Greenland homes made of turf and rock, as well as a modern hunters' shack built of wood and corrugated iron. Unrusted fuel containers and heaps of beer cans testified that hunters had been there recently.

Inside, the shack was surprisingly tidy, with its small kitchen, rough-hewn table, and half a dozen bunks. The larder contained an emergency cache of pemmican, soda crackers, and paraffin. The single incongruous wall decoration was a tattered old poster for a Charles Bronson film in Danish. Qav translated the title: "Sweet Revenge."

There was a brief discussion about whether to move the group's sleeping quarters ashore. Everyone agreed to stay on the boat but to transfer the bulky gear, including the Icehawk and extra food, to the shack.

After dinner Dansgaard called a meeting in the galley.

"Tomorrow Anaq and I will set out. We will each tow an extra kayak with enough food and gear for ten days. It will take three or four hours to reach the Puisortoq glacier; another four hours—God willing—to traverse its sea edge. Using the fixed ropes from our last trip, we should reach the Norse house a few hours later." Dansgaard laughed. "But remember—I, at least, am an old man, so we may move slower than we expect."

"Will you be in radio contact?" Julia asked nervously. The expedition had brought three different kinds of high-tech communications gear.

"We will try to check in every fifteen minutes, except, of course, when we are climbing the cliff face. If everything goes OK, we'll spend our first day in the valley reconnoitering the area around the house. The second day we'll begin to move up the valley. If we see any evidence of the mammoths, we'll signal you to launch the Icehawk. How long will it take, Jack?"

"Once you send us coordinates," Jack replied, "it will take only a few minutes to put it in the air. It should be over the valley in less than an hour."

"How long can it stay aloft?" Dansgaard asked.

"If there is bright sun, like today, to charge its solar panels, at least five hours, depending on the wind patterns."

"Excellent." Dansgaard smiled.

"How does the remote control work?" asked Julia.

"Watch this." Jack swivelled in his chair to face three laptops sitting in a row along the galley table. He punched a few keys, and all three brightened to life. "The first PC plots the location of the Icehawk in flight on a three-dimensional map grid. The second displays the picture from the telecam in its nose, and the third will relay the picture from Dansgaard's handheld camera as soon as the trike is within fifteen or twenty air miles of his location."

It took several minutes for Qav, aided by Dansgaard, to translate all this for Anaq. The old hunter shook his head. "Too complicated!" he sighed.

Jack laughed. "The system is actually even more complex—not only can I receive pictures from the Icehawk and Dr. Dansgaard simultaneously, but I can also broadcast the aerial images and their GPS coordinates to the Professor on the ground." Jack picked up the fantastic-looking videocam and pointed out its two screens.

"State of the art," cooed Julia, awed.

"Well, not quite," said Jack, blushing. "But it is the next best thing to having our own satellite overhead. If the mammoths truly exist, we will find them within a few hours."

Dansgaard put his arm around Jack. "Now listen, kids. This is the important part. While Anaq and I are gone, Jack will be expedition leader and Julia will be second in command."

The younger boys gave sour looks. "Ageism," Conor muttered under his breath.

"But these two will be in charge of the boat. They are our sailors. In any emergency, it will be up to Qav and Conor to return you safely to Tasiilaq." The duo's faces brightened at Dansgaard's praise.

But Julia remained troubled. "What are we supposed to do in an emergency? Say, if for some reason, we lost radio contact with you?"

Dansgaard pulled a thick envelope from the pocket of his anorak. He handed it to Jack. "This is to be opened only in case of an emergency. It contains my instructions on how to deal with any possible contingency." The professor then turned toward the others. "Jack will be in charge, and you must all promise to obey him."

Dansgaard looked each of them sternly in the face. Qav winced and Conor gulped. Jack's leadership was uncontroversial, but the kids were uneasy with the idea of secret written orders. It seemed ominous.

"Don't look so gloomy," Dansgaard reassured them. "Nothing is going to happen to Anaq and me, except perhaps the discovery of the century. And you will be its real heroes. Now off to bed. We all rise at 5 A.M."

Later that night Jack had another of his strange dreams. He was on the Inland Ice. In the distance, Conor was crying for help, but every time Jack ran in the direction of his voice it stopped, then resumed from an entirely different direction. Finally Conor's cries became louder and louder, coming now from all sides.

Jack woke up covered with sweat and shaking. After he calmed down a bit, he got up for a glass of water, being careful not to wake the others. On his way back from the galley he peered through the half-open door into the other cabin. Anaq was asleep, but Dansgaard was awake. He sat at a small desk with his back to Jack, holding a photograph of a young woman: his long-dead wife.

By 6 A.M. Dansgaard and Anaq were already out of sight, paddling briskly toward the terrors of Puisortoq.

Before they left Anaq had taken Qav aside for a talk. When he was through, Anaq smiled and gave Qav, near tears, a long hug. Turning towards the others, he squatted low on his haunches and contorted his face into a terrifying expression. Raising his hands above his head like a comic monster, he lunged toward each of them in turn while chanting what seemed like terrible curses. The kids were quite taken aback. Then, just as suddenly as he started, Anaq stopped and smiled benignly.

Dansgaard laughed as he climbed into his kayak. "Anaq has just ordered your personal spirit guardians to take care of you and make sure you obey our orders to stay in camp. If I were you, I wouldn't defy him."

Three hours after their departure, a little behind schedule, Dansgaard radioed that they were on the edge of Puisortoq. The kids crowded around the receiver as Jack talked to Dansgaard.

"Dr. Dansgaard, are you sure you want to proceed?"

"Don't worry, Jack," said the slightly crackly voice over the receiver. "The sea is very calm and there is little ice. We are almost a mile off-shore for safety. We will now paddle as hard as we can in the hopes of clearing the danger area within three hours. I'll radio when we're clear. Be sure to feed Anori."

Normally the rough sea and myriad icebergs force those who dare Puisortoq to stay closer to the ice edge, so it was good news that Dansgaard and Anaq were able to skirt the monster at a greater distance. Still, the kids were at the edge of their seats for the next several hours.

Finally, just after midday Dansgaard announced triumphantly: "We've done it. We are past the danger zone without any problem. Please put Julia on."

Jack got up so Julia could speak. "Yes, Dr. Dansgaard?"

"Julia, I thought you would like to know that we saw a polar bear sunning itself on an ice shelf."

Julia was excited. "Fantastic. But strange to see one this far south in August or in such a dangerous locality."

"Don't worry, my dear," Dansgaard replied softly. "He seemed to be both fat and happy. Hardly bothered to blink as we paddled by. Now put Jack back on."

"Jack," Dansgaard continued, "for the next few hours Anaq and I will be absorbed in the tedious tasks of securing our kayaks and scaling the cliff face. Don't worry if you don't hear from me. But let's talk again at 7 P.M.—we should be comfortably ensconced in the old Viking house by then. Over and out."

The kids nervously waited for the next message. Jack radioed the government house in Tassilaq to confirm their safe arrival in Tingmiarmiut without saying anything about the expedition's real objective. He checked the weather reports: fine prospects for tomorrow.

Qav, meanwhile, decided to share something with Conor and Julia. It was a popular legend on the east coast. It had even found its way into print, and he summarized for them a passage from a book he had recently bought in Copenhagen:

> The American author Lawrence Millman had visited East Greenland sometime in the late 1980s. He met the veteran hunter Avannag, who told him of the strange signs of a reclusive, possibly lost culture living in the recesses of the very coast where they were anchored.
>
> "All evidence seemed to point to a band of Stone Age hunters still living somewhere in these isolated fjords, a little nomadic scattering of people who had apparently never met any of their own latter-day countrymen. The survival of such a band was quite possible, Avannaq said, because almost no one had ever gone to that stretch of coast until Skjoldungen was founded in 1938."[13]

Qav explained that this "lost tribe" hypothesis was seriously accepted by most local hunters, although his father dismissed it as part of the folklore of the "Dead Land." Conor asked what Anaq thought.

"Oh, he just smiles enigmatically and refuses to say anything," chuckled Qav. "I think he half believes his grandfather is leader of the mystery band."

"Well, *someone* roofed the Norse house and slaughtered a mammoth," Julia emphasized.

Jack interrupted. He had picked up Dansgaard, although the signal this time was much fainter.

29. CAPTURED!

"Jack, can you hear me?" Dansgaard's voice sounded oddly strained. Jack turned up the volume so everyone could hear.

"Yes, Professor. The reception is fainter but still clear. Is everything OK? Are you in the Norse house?"

"We are in the Norse camp."

"Norse camp?" Jack was confused.

"Jack, listen very carefully. A contingency has arisen which I never anticipated. Something of staggering significance. It may be several days before I am able to contact you again or fully explain what has happened. At all costs, you must keep everyone in camp. Do you understand?"

"Wait, Professor . . ."

"Jack, do what I say—no questions! They are returning, and I must go off the air."

"Who are 'they,' Professor? What's going on?"

"Jack, we are captives . . ." Suddenly there was commotion at the other end, and Jack heard harsh commands shouted in a language he didn't understand. Then Dansgaard's radio went silent.

Everyone was stunned.

"Captives?" asked Julia.

Jack turned to Qav. "Did you understand what that strange voice was saying?"

Qav was white. "I think it was some absolutely weird dialect of Icelandic or Danish. All I could make out were the words for 'witchcraft' and 'eternal sleep.'"

Jack gulped.

Conor, flushed with excitement, now spoke up. "Jack, we must rescue them. Qav and I are incredibly fast kayakers—we can reach them in four or five hours. If you launch the Icehawk we can send you images, and . . ."

"Conor!" Jack was trembling with anger. "Stop it! Under no condition are you and Qav to leave this camp." Jack turned his back to the others and took out Dansgaard's envelope. He opened it, and after a few moments, began to read aloud.

"If any unforeseen emergency arises and you lose contact with us, you are to remain in camp for three days monitoring the radio. If you hear nothing, break camp and return to Tasiilaq. Tell the authorities that Anaq and I have disappeared while exploring the edge of Puisortoq."

"That's the Professor's order, and that's what we will do. As much as we may dislike it, we wait here," Jack's tone was authoritative.

Conor was biting his lip, Qav had his head bowed, and Julia was visibly shaken. Jack felt ashamed as having to become such a terrible tyrant.

"Look, guys, I'm sorry. I know we've always been comrades and decided things democratically, but now I have to follow Dansgaard's orders. It's for your safety."

Qav lifted his head. "Jack, my grandfather and Dansgaard are in terrible peril. How will I look back years from now, knowing that I did nothing to save them?" Conor nodded his approval.

"Yes, Jack," Julia piped in, "there must be something we can do."

Jack felt trapped, but he knew his responsibility. "No, not right now. I want everyone to busy themselves doing something useful. We'll take shifts monitoring the radio. Conor, you're on first. Julia and Qav, help me with the Icehawk—if we don't hear from Dansgaard in twenty-four hours, I'll send it on a reconnaissance flight."

The hours passed with agonizing slowness. There was no message from Dansgaard, just sinister static. The kids, tired after the longest day of their lives, began to drift off into short, troubled sleeps. Jack was the last to nap.

He woke up suddenly—Anori was licking his face. Across the cabin, Julia was curled up asleep in her bunk, with her polar bear pendant in her hand. Jack stood up, yawned, and stretched his arms. Suddenly he realized: Where were Conor and Qav?

It took less than a minute to search the boat. Jack bolted ashore with Anori behind him: perhaps the boys were in the shack with their kayaks. He swung open the heavy winter door. The Icehawk was there, but the kayaks were gone. Jack clenched his fists.

"Jack! Jack!" Julia was shouting from the boat, tears streaming down her face. She held a note she'd found on Conor's bed.

> *Dear Jack and Julia. We can't leave the old guys in such danger. We have gone to rescue them. Don't worry. We'll radio you when we reach the Valley of the Runes. C and Q*

Jack was beside himself. "The idiots! The brave little fools!" Julia put her arm around him, and after a minute Jack composed himself. Whatever it took, he and Julia would now have to rescue the rescuers.

30. CONOR'S ESKIMO ROLL

"Conor," Qav urged in a soft whisper, "stay next to me."

It was still "night," or rather, the three hours of dusk that passed for night this time of year in southeastern Greenland. To make better time, Qav and Conor were skirting the very edge of Puisortoq, about a hundred yards from the towering ice cliff.

Behind his kayak Qav towed two of the boat's life preservers rigged into a float for Conor's infrasound detector in its waterproof container. He also had his grandfather's ancient .300 Savage rifle tied on. Conor had a backpack with extra food strapped on the front of his kayak.

As Conor pulled next to Qav, the terrifying ice mountain began to groan. The eerie sound chilled their bones to the marrow. Then, to their horror, they watched a large cornice of ice—the size of a house—plunge hundreds of feet into the sea ahead of them. It reminded Conor of an artist's conception of an icy comet hitting the ocean.

The sea seemed to explode: first, huge vertical geysers of spray shot up, then a small tsunami headed straight for them. Both boys braced themselves and closed their eyes. The impact was like being hit by a train.

Qav's kayak literally became airborne. When he splashed down, the sea was churning chaos. Using desperate sculling brace strokes, he was miraculously able to keep upright. But where was Conor?

Qav suddenly saw Conor's upside-down kayak. "Conor!" he screamed.

Immediately, as if in response to Qav's cry, Conor's kayak rolled upright. Qav paddled over to his friend. To his incredulity, Conor—having executed a perfect "Eskimo roll"—was laughing.

"Boy, Qav, that was the thrill of a lifetime. Super cool."

"Conor," scolded Qav, "you're an Irish madman."

As the sea gradually settled, they checked their gear for damage. The infrasound detector and the rifle were no worse for the experience, but Conor's backpack was waterlogged and some of the rations turned into soup. They would have to tighten their belts.

"OK, Qav," Conor urged, "let's get going."

Qav had to admit that Conor's insane good humor took the edge off what otherwise had been a terrifying experience, but neither boy had any desire to stick around admiring their good fortune.

Qav paddled like an Olympic champion and Conor managed to stay right behind. There was a monstrous ice overhang ahead, so they headed seaward to put a few hundred more feet between them and the world's most dangerous glacier.

Two hours later, with the sun again in the sky, they arrived at their destination. It was just as Dansgaard had described: A magnificent waterfall plunged into the sea from a cliff fissured with cracks and crevices. A diagonal couloir, which crossed the back of the waterfall, offered an obvious route to the top.

The climbing looked fairly simple, especially with the fixed ropes left by Dansgaard and Anaq. The boys' real problem was getting their kayaks on shore. It was low tide, and the narrow shelf along the base of the cliff was now six to eight feet above them. It took them almost an hour to hoist the kayaks and their gear out of the water.

Dansgaard's and Anaq's kayaks were wedged upright inside the base of the couloir, and it took only a few minutes for the boys to stow their kayaks as well. Since their arms were aching from their marathon sea race across Puisortoq, they decided to eat and rest for a half hour.

"Conor, shouldn't we radio Jack and Julia now?" Qav asked.

"Yeah, I almost forgot." He removed his waterproof *tuiitsoq*, the traditional kayaking jacket. Both he and Qav wore shoulder holsters, which, instead of holding revolvers, held what looked like cellular phones. They were state-of-the-art Garmin Super-Rinos: shortwave radios, walkie-talkies, miniature video cameras, and GPS receivers in one.

Conor tuned his to the base-camp frequency. "Jack, can you read me? Jack, are you there?"

"Conor? This is Julia. I can hear you clearly. I'll get Jack."

A minute later: "Conor, for godsakes, where are you?"

"Jack, calm down. We're fine. We're at the base of the cliff. The climbing route is easy, and there are fixed ropes to help us hoist our gear. We should be on top within an hour."

"Conor, you listen to me. Do not—I repeat—do not attempt to ascend the cliff. Shelter in the couloir and I'll radio Tasiilaq for the Coast Guard to rescue you. I don't want you and Qav pursuing Dansgaard, and I don't want you risking Puisortoq again. Stay where you are and I'll have a helicopter there within a few hours."

"Jack, if you call Tasiilaq, Dansgaard's secret will be world news. Aside from possibly endangering him and Anaq, it would ensure an ecological disaster. Dansgaard was right. The world isn't ready yet for the mammoths or for whatever strange humans may also inhabit the valley."

"Conor." Jack was shouting into the radio. "My concern is saving you and Qav. We have no idea what's happened to the Professor and Anaq, who may have captured them, or what terrors may exist in that damn valley. I want you two to sit down and wait to be rescued."

Conor looked at Qav. "Conor, tell Jack we have to climb this cliff. We have to find out what's happened to my grandad and Dansgaard." Conor nodded.

"Look, Jack, I'm sorry, but we have to keep going. But I promise we will be as stealthy as ninjas. We'll reconnoiter the Norse house, but we won't go any further. I'll give you a blow by blow on the radio. We'll stay in constant contact. Then we'll climb back down."

"No, Conor, absolutely not," Jack sounded panicky.

"Love you, bro," said Conor guiltily, and then he turned his Garmin off.

"Let's get climbing," he said to Qav.

32. A MAMMOTH SURPRISE

"Piece of cake," Conor whispered to Qav as they neared the top of the couloir.

"Yeah, but now we need to become invisible," Qav whispered.

Leaving all their gear except the rifle hidden in the mouth of the couloir, the two boys slowly lifted their heads above the surface, then crawled on their bellies like commandos. They were stunned by the lush greenness of the valley. The tussock and dwarf willow were soon high enough to conceal them as they scrambled forward in a crouch. After about a hundred yards, they took shelter behind some large boulders. Qav pulled out a powerful pair of pocket binoculars and began to scan the landscape.

The Norse house was visible on a ledge above a stream about a half mile away. Qav watched it for almost five minutes.

"It looks deserted," he whispered to Conor.

"OK, let's bring our gear up here. This is a good concealed location for a camp."

They quickly retrieved their gear and erected their mountaineering tent in the shadow of one of the huge boulders, which were "glacial erratics" that had been deposited by an ice sheet. Then, with Qav carrying his grandfather's rifle and Conor with his infrasound detector in his backpack, they carefully moved forward. They stopped every hundred yards or so to scan the way ahead with the binoculars. There was no evidence of any danger.

The Norse house was even more impressive than in Dansgaard's photographs, with its massive stone walls and its roof constructed of what appeared to be driftwood beams and turf.

Qav chambered a round in his rifle as they approached the doorway. Someone had recently fitted a crude, massive door made from a modern ship's hatch. There were no hinges, so Qav had to give Conor a hand to shift it aside.

The house was dark and musty smelling. It consisted of one large room with a sleeping platform on three sides and a stone chimney. Qav shuddered and thought to himself that compared to the snug, seal oil-heated dwellings of the old Greenlanders, this would be an icehouse during the winter.

Dansgaard's and Anaq's gear was neatly arranged near the doorway. There was no sign of any struggle or violence, although outside the house the trampled grass testified to recent visitors.

"Let's put the door back in place and see if we can follow the tracks," Qav suggested. Conor remembered his last promise to Jack but nodded anyway.

Qav had no difficulty finding the track and following it upstream. Although he lacked his grandfather's expertise, he estimated that there was a group of about ten or twelve people traveling together. After they'd walked for about a half hour, the track descended to where the stream flowed through a large flower-filled meadow.

Conor tapped Qav on the shoulder.

"What do you think about this vegetation?"

"Different from Tasiilaq." Qav studied the landscape closely. "The individual species are familiar, but their abundance and overall composition are odd. If this were a botany exam, I'd guess we're looking at a different plant community."

"Exactly. This is what Ice Age paleontologists call a classic 'Mammoth Steppe.' The landscape is the result of heavy grazing followed by equally heavy manuring. The mammoths themselves have cultivated this unique plant community. The only other extant example is Wrangel Island."[14]

Qav suddenly gasped. "Look over there."

The faint trail of the captives had intersected a far more dramatic track that looked as if it had been made by a herd of very large and heavy animals—Mammoth Steppe, indeed.

Within a few minutes Conor had found dozens of clearly outlined footprints in the mud. "*Mammuthus primigenius,* but a dwarf subspecies, probably half the stature of their original ancestors. And look here, Qav!"

Conor had found some long reddish-brown hairs snagged on a sharp willow twig.

"No, look at *this,*" Qav replied.

It was a large mammoth dropping. Qav gingerly touched it. "Still a bit warm. Maybe a few hours old."

Conor handed Qav his digital camera. "Document this while I set up the infrasound detector." Conor found a conveniently flat boulder, pulled out the tiny dishlike antenna, and mounted it on a small tripod. He put on the headphones. His expression of intense concentration soon became an ear-to-ear grin.

"Here, Qav, listen to this." Conor helped Qav adjust the headphones. The amplified infrasound was a combination of rumbling and a deep groaning.

"Incredible."

"The rangefinder," Conor explained, "indicates the herd to be about three thousand meters directly upstream."

"Let's call Jack and Julia," reminded Qav.

33. A HEAVY RESPONSIBILITY

Jack was tearing his heart out over Conor and Qav. Julia tried to console him.

"Look, Jack, they have a rifle, and Qav is a Greenlander, an expert outdoorsman. I'm sure they're alright for now."

"Julia, you don't know Conor. If he finds the mammoths, he'll go bonkers and never return. As I see it, I have two choices: radio Tasiilaq for help or go after them myself. Obviously, the responsible route is to call the authorities."

Julia was horrified at the thought of the world descending upon Dansgaard's secret valley. "No, Jack, please don't call Tasiilaq. Aside from breaking our word to the Professor, it would take too long for the Greenlandic government to send a rescue party. Let's you and I rescue them." Julia smiled at the thought of adventure.

Jack was incredulous. "What do you mean, 'you and I'? Has everyone gone mad? I am not letting you leave this base. Someone has to stay here to maintain radio contact with Tasiilaq. Do you understand?"

Julia fumed. "Jack, this outrageous male chauvinism . . ." Before the argument could develop further, the radio came to life.

"Jack, Julia, can you read me?" It was Conor.

"Conor, where are you?"

Conor told Jack and Julia of their progress so far, including the amazing discovery of a mammoth herd just a mile away.

"Conor," Jack barked, "this is totally out of hand. Are you trying to rescue Dansgaard and Anaq or chase mammoths?"

Conor realized that Jack had a point. "No, don't worry, the old guys are our priority."

"I don't suppose you would heed me if I ordered you and Qav to come back?"

"Sorry, Jack."

Jack realized that it was impossible to oppose Conor's irresistible curiosity or Qav's devotion to his grandfather. "OK, Conor, get this. You guys are probably headed straight into an ambush. If Anaq, one of the greatest hunters in the Arctic, can end up as a captive, you're unlikely to do much better."

"OK, what do you propose?" Now Qav was on the air as well.

"Return to the Norse house and I'll meet you there in the Icehawk. The weather is still great, so I estimate a flight time of little more than an hour. Set your Garmins to automatic transmission mode and I'll use them as a homing signal. OK?"

Now it was Conor's turn to fruitlessly implore his brother. "No, Jack, don't do that. You've never flown the Icehawk. Even if you manage to take off, you have to fly over Puisortoq. If you had to crash-land, you would never be able to escape. Please, Jack, stay put. We're fine."

"Well, Conor," Jack said coolly, "now the shoe's on the other foot. If you're going to foolishly walk into the mouth of danger, I'm going to be there with you. Whether you want me to or not. Now, do you understand the plan?"

Conor cast a horrified look at Qav. "OK, Jack, if you want to come, take the boat, stay far out to sea, and avoid Puisortoq. We'll meet you at the base of the waterfall."

"Sorry, Conor, but I'm not sure I can navigate the boat. You're the sailor in the family, and besides, it would take too long. I'll be airborne in about fifteen minutes. I'm coming to get you—watch out."

Conor realized that there was nothing he could say to dissuade Jack. "OK, big brother, we'll be waiting at the Norse house. But please be careful."

Up to this point Julia had been the bystander as all five males had plunged recklessly ahead into unforeseen dangers. It was now time to put her foot down, and she proceeded to read Jack the riot act.

"I'm tired of being ordered around. I'm less foolish than any of you, and I've certainly have had more wilderness experience than either you or Conor. If you leave me behind, I'll take the boat and head down the coast by myself." Julia was adamant.

"But, Julia," Jack stumbled. "You don't know how to operate the boat any more than I do."

"I don't care, Jack." she crossed her arms defiantly. "If you don't take me with you on the Icehawk, I'll try my own luck on the boat."

Jack was beginning to think he was going crazy.

"But Julia," he responded weakly, "there's only room for one on the Icehawk."

"Nonsense. You yourself told me that you had designed it to carry both you and Conor, and I weigh less than he does. Let's get going."

Jack thought to himself, "Not even Conor is *this* stubborn."

Finally, he gave in. "Since everyone else has managed to run off and get themselves in trouble, I suppose it would be unfair to leave you behind in perfect safety. But do you clearly understand the danger involved? The Icehawk is entirely experimental, and we'll be flying over some of the most dangerous terrain in the world."

Julia smiled in triumph.

"How much food shall I take?" she asked matter-of-factly.

"None," replied Jack. "We can't risk any additional weight."

"How about my little backpack? I really need a few things."

"OK, but keep it to an absolute minimum. Now help me put the skis on the Icehawk; we'll launch it from the fjord."

They left out plenty of water and food for Anori, who would guard the boat while they were gone. Since the atmosphere above Puisortoq would be freezing, they dressed in winter parkas. Jack helped Julia put on the rock climber's harness that would secure her to the frame of the Icehawk. They each carried a Garmin communicator, a flashlight, and a small icepick.

After folding up the wheels and attaching the skis, they easily maneuvered the Icehawk into the water alongside the small dock. While Jack steadied the craft, Julia climbed in, and then he followed. After making sure Julia was securely harnessed, he started the little engine.

The propeller began to turn and was soon whirling invisibly. "Twenty revs per second," Jack told Julia. The little plane was straining to fly. "Not too late to back out."

Julia smiled defiantly. "Let 'er rip," she yelled. He handed her a light Kevlar helmet similar to the kind worn by cyclists. It was equipped with built-in earphones and a tiny microphone connected to the Garmin, which would allow her to talk to Jack in flight as well as to Qav and Conor on the ground.

Jack did one final safety check. He suddenly remembered a favorite photograph in an old book: Charles Lindbergh and his young bride, Anne Morrow, at Tasiilaq in 1933 after a pioneer flight across the Inland Ice. He realized that his trike weighed less than one of the propellers on Lindy's big Lockheed Sirius seaplane.

He pushed the throttle forward. The little plane skated across the water, past the bow of the boat. He pulled back on the control bar. The Icehawk hesitated for a second, then soared. Its gossamer wings provided a surprisingly powerful lift. Julia, her hands resting on Jack's shoulders, gave him a squeeze. She was thrilled.

Jack headed out to sea and along the coast until he had built up enough altitude, then headed straight for Cape Bille and the dreaded ice cliffs of Puisortoq.

EPISODE SIX: *The Captives of Time*

Qav and Conor silently made their way back toward the Norse house. Conor was feeling miserable about Jack's dangerous flight across Puisortoq; the more he fretted, the guiltier he felt about putting his brother in peril. It had been idiotic to think that Jack—his protective and always responsible big brother—would quietly wait at base camp while Conor and Qav plunged into mad adventure. Moreover, knowing Julia, she was probably also defying death right now with Jack.

Qav suddenly gave a hand signal to halt. Following his example, Conor quietly dropped to his knees, then flattened himself on the ground. Qav raised himself on his elbows and squinted intensely through his binoculars. After a minute, he let Conor have a peek.

The Norse house was a quarter mile ahead, but there was a new and very strange-looking visitor in front of it. He was an adult, short in stature but very powerfully built, wearing a leather tunic and breeches, and some kind of fur cape. He was on one knee, carefully studying the ground—obviously, he had discovered the boys' footprints.

Then the stranger looked up, and Conor shuddered. His face was painted chalky white, and there were hideous red circles drawn around his eyes. He looked like a monstrous clown. Conor nervously handed the binoculars back to Qav.

Qav also trembled at the savage visage. He motioned Conor to crawl closer and whispered: "The welcoming committee is even weirder than I expected."

"It looks like they have Halloween all year round," quipped Conor.

Qav was once again reassured by his friend's gutsiness. Then he outlined a rapid-fire plan.

"Well, the bad news is that he is coming this way. The good news is that he hasn't seen us or discovered our gear. We can't leave a trail for him to follow, so we need to double back to the stream. We'll head down the water a half mile or so, then cut back toward the boulders and our stuff. By that time, Jack should be overhead."

Conor nodded agreement, and the boys rapidly retraced their steps, moving in a half-crouch well camouflaged by vegetation. At the stream, they turned right, back toward the coast. They were sheltered by high eroded banks and kept strictly to the stream cobble to avoid leaving any telltale footprints. The stream, surprisingly, was almost lukewarm, with hints of sulfur, but the two boys had no time to ponder the curious phenomena.

After a few hundred meters, they stopped. Qav unshouldered his grandfather's rifle. Crouching behind a lichen-stained boulder, they waited nervously to see if anyone followed. Nothing. Qav then crawled up the embankment to scan behind them with his binoculars. Still nothing.

"It looks OK, Conor. He seems to have gone upstream or perhaps returned to the Norse house to wait for us. Let's go on a few hundred meters more downstream, then go to the boulder camp."

They continued forward until they heard the roar of the distant waterfall where the stream flung itself into the sea. Warily, they climbed out of the creekbed and crawled through the dwarf willow and larch until they were back in the shelter of the boulders. They were reassured to be so close to the cliff face and a quick retreat by sea if necessary.

While Qav kept a vigilant lookout, rifle in hand, Conor tried to radio the Icehawk. His heart was in his throat. "Please, please, Jack," he murmured, "answer me."

36. THE HAWK SOARS

It took ten minutes for the Icehawk, spiraling over the ocean, to build enough altitude to surmount the razorlike peaks that ringed Tingmiarmiut. Although it was a mild day, the perennial avalanche of cold air off the ice sheet collided with warmer coastal summer air to create chaotic eddies. The delicate Icehawk, exquisitely sensitive to air motion, alternately dipped, soared, and tumbled.

Julia worried for a moment that their wings might be torn off by the vortex, but when she looked at Jack, she realized that he was in a rapturous trance. He was fully in control of his little plane. Indeed, it responded perfectly to every nuance of command. Like the fearless raptor for which it had been named, the Icehawk exulted in its wild freedom.

Catching a particularly powerful updraft, it bolted over the alpine barrier. Julia felt as if she were in an elevator shooting upward at a hundred miles per hour. They came so close to the highest of the peaks that she was almost tempted to stick out her hand and scoop snow from its summit.

The Icehawk dropped sharply on the other side. Julia was almost blinded by the intense reflection from the glacier. She pulled down her dark ice goggles. Ahead of them was the white nightmare of Puisortoq. Its surface was fissured into thousands of deep, perhaps bottomless crevasses. Sinister shards of ice, like deadly sharks' teeth, were randomly strewn everywhere. A crash landing here was unthinkable. She looked again to Jack for reassurance.

He was still smiling. "Don't worry. This will be easy. Puisortoq is reflecting lots of high-energy sunlight into the Icehawk's solar panels."

Jack was right. Although at times almost blown sideways by the glacial downslope winds, the Icehawk gamely kept her altitude. Within twenty minutes they were in sight of the rugged granite ramparts that formed the ice monster's southern wall.

Jack gulped. It was the same black mountain ridge that he had seen in his dream.

Suddenly, there was static in the earphones, then Conor's desperate plea.

"Jack, come in. Come in. Do you read me?"

"Hey, little brother."

"Wow, you're OK. I was so worried."

Conor's relief was so touching that Jack resisted the impulse to scold him again for instigating this whole mess. After all, Jack had finally gotten to fly the Icehawk.

"No, relax. We've almost finished crossing Puisortoq. The plane is handling brilliantly. And I have a tourist along."

Julia punched Jack in the back.

"So what do you have to report?" Jack asked his brother.

"Mammoths and killer clowns," blurted Conor.

"What? Come again?"

"We located a herd of pygmy mammoths on the infrasound detector. About three kilometers up valley from the Norse house."

"Wow, that's great. But what do you mean 'killer clowns'? Are you joking?"

Now Qav was on the radio.

"Qav here. We saw one of the locals. A hunter with a strangely painted face."

"But did he see *you?*" Jack was worried again.

"No, but he found our footprints. We backtracked and evaded him. We're well concealed in a castlelike formation of large boulders near the cliff face, south of the stream."

"Can I land near there?"

"Absolutely. There is a soft meadow without any large rocks a hundred meters from our tent. Are you reading our homing signal?"

"Yeah. It's very clear. Now listen, we're nearly to the edge of the valley. I'm going to circle over it for ten or fifteen minutes. I'll try to locate the encampment where they have taken Anaq and Dansgaard. I'll download the topography to your GPS function. OK?"

Jack meant that he would use the video camera in the nose of the Icehawk to relay digital images to Qav and Conor's Garmins. This would provide them with a clear display of their position in relationship to landforms and landmarks like the Norse house, thus making it easier to avoid the Halloween monster.

"Thanks, Jack, that will be a great help. Signal again when you approach for a landing. We'll make sure you have a safe welcome." Qav thought of mentioning his grandfather's rifle but realized it might cause more consternation than reassurance.

"That's grand," replied Jack. "Now turn on your Garmin displays and you'll see what we see."

Jack's controls for flying the Icehawk included a small "mouse," controlled by his right index finger, which allowed him to swivel the plane's video camera in any direction. As he cleared the rocky southern ridge of Puisortoq, he switched the video on.

Immediately the displays on Qav's and Conor's Garmins came to life in vivid color. Images of ice and dark rock yielded to the startling green of the valley below. Looking up from their miniature television screens, the two boys could see a glint of sunlight reflected from the solar panels of the Icehawk's wings a mile away and perhaps a thousand feet in the air.

Jack and Julia gasped in awe at the landscape beneath them. Dansgaard's "mystery valley" was actually only one of a half-dozen green and ice free canyons radiating like fingers of a giant hand from a maternal labyrinth of smaller, higher, and partially glaciated valleys and sawtooth peaks. Although elsewhere the day was bright and clear, there were foglike patches over parts of the valleys. Jack surmised that they were evidence of hydrothermal activity.

"Do you see the fog?" Jack was now talking to Qav and Conor on the ground as well as to Julia behind him. "Could it be steam?"

"Hot springs and geysers," agreed Conor. "When the wind is stronger, the steam clouds probably obscure most of the terrain. It insulates the valleys from the cold and keeps them well hidden most of the time."

"Great camouflage for a mammoth refugia," said Julia.

"This complex of valleys is much larger than we suspected." Qav was worried as he studied the aerial images on his Garmin. "What if the kidnappers have already moved my grandfather and Dansgaard into one of the lateral valleys? It could take weeks to search out every nook and cranny."

"Well, let's take it one valley at a time. Julia and I are going to fly over your heads, then straight up the valley and back. We should at least be able to locate the mammoths and your Halloween friend. OK?"

"Roger."

Jack sharply dipped the wings to the left and guided the Icehawk into a slow arc of descent, passing a few hundred feet over the heads of Qav and Conor. Julia scanned the ground below with a powerful pair of Zeiss mini-binoculars. Jack circled the Norse house.

Suddenly, someone came out of the door—it was the man with the painted face. He shouted at the Icehawk and waved his arms, then as Jack dropped lower for a closer look, he bolted in panic. Jack started to pursue him, but Julia warned, "No, Jack. Don't scare him."

Jack powered up for altitude. "You're right, Julia. We don't want these people to think we're extraterrestrial monsters."

Jack angled off, but the figure on the ground was still running flat out, obviously in mortal terror. Jack took the Icehawk back to the ridgeline so that they maintained a clear view of the man but were no longer in obvious pursuit.

"We're going to track him from here. Hopefully he will take us to Dansgaard and Anaq."

On the ground, Qav and Conor sighed in relief that their pursuer was now the pursued. At the same time, they felt a twinge of guilt. After all, they were the intruders. What right did they have to come crashing into anyone's refugia or Shangri-la? Or to chase one of the locals like a scared rabbit?

"Conor, are you there?"

"Yeah, Jack."

"Can you see him now?"

"No, the image is too small to make out. What's happening?"

"He's crossed the stream, still running. But there's a fog patch ahead. He's headed straight toward it. We may lose him."

Jack brought the Icehawk lower, but within a few minutes the strange painted man had disappeared into the fog. Through a break in the mist, however, he and Julia did catch a startling glimpse of a boiling terrace, the steps of which were ocher and orange.

"Confirm hydrothermal activity. There's a large complex of hot springs directly below us."

The Icehawk continued its reconnaisance. The fog dissipated, and they could see that the valley broadened to a maximum width of about six miles. There were several small lakes.

"Conor, this one is for you." Jack put the Icehawk into a dive.

As Conor peered at his Garmin, he could discern several dark moving dots in the meadow. The hair on his neck stood up. As the Icehawk descended, the figures grew larger and clearer on the screen. It was the pygmy mammoth herd.

"Wow!" gasped all four kids, simultaneously.

"Careful. Don't scare them, Jack," Conor's voice was soft, almost reverential.

Jack nosed the plane up and slowly circled above the curious but unpanicked herd.

Julia told Conor that she counted three mature females, a young male, and five calves.

He had already done a quick calculation. "Julia, with a rough surface area of 150 square miles of forage in this valley complex, I estimate maybe fifty in all, with six bulls."

"That's pretty close to my guess, too, Conor. Although I'd make the upper limit seventy-five, with ten bulls."

"Is that a lot?" Qav asked.

Conor answered. "Well, the ecosystem is considerably larger than the Channel Islands of Southern California where a unique subspecies of dwarf Columbian mammoths thrived during the Glacial Maximum. On the other hand, a population this small tends to undergo genetic degeneration. Defects become magnified by inbreeding, and current theory suggests that they shouldn't have survived this long. But I guess we'll have to rewrite the textbook, won't we, Julia?"

"I guess so." Julia was utterly captivated by the scene below.

Jack interrupted the reverie. "OK. I'll fly ahead a little further."

The last six miles of the valley led to a low saddle that crossed over to the next valley south, as well as to a maze of steeper, narrower canyons incised in the surrounding mountains—"box canyons" in the parlance of the American West.

Jack and Julia scrutinized this area very carefully, descending at one point to less than a hundred feet, but there was no evidence of humans or their habitation.

"Any sign of my grandfather?" Qav was delighted by the mammoths, but he would have preferred to have seen Anaq.

"Sorry, nothing at all. If there is a village, it is probably hidden by the fog. I'm going to turn around. Before we explore further, we need to have a summit conference and decide upon a new strategy."

"OK, come home."

As the Icehawk turned back toward Qav and Conor, Jack could see a thin gray cloudline to the west. A weather system was predicted to move into southeastern Greenland sometime during the night and persist for a day or so. Flying would be impossible.

Fifteen minutes later, Jack was on the ground explaining the situation to his worried comrades.

"So we're stuck here for at least twenty-four hours, unable to either fly or use the kayaks. Fortunately we have the Norse house to shelter ourselves and the Icehawk."

"Um, maybe Conor and I should sleep out here, in our tent." Qav sounded nervous.

The others laughed. "Come on, Qav, let's stick together."

"I know, but that old Viking pile is too creepy. None of my ancestors would have set foot in it. And besides, that's where my grandfather and Dansgaard were captured."

"Maybe Qav has a point," ventured Julia, a little apprehensive herself.

"Well, I am afraid we don't have much choice," countered Jack. "And perhaps being captured is our only option for saving Anaq and Dansgaard." He smiled placidly.

The other kids were startled by Jack's nonchalance at the prospect of being involuntary guests at a Halloween party. But he was right: what other choice did they have but to spend a long night in that ghostly place?

38. THE GUN DEBATE

"Night," of course, is greatly abbreviated just south of the Arctic Circle in early August, with only a few hours of dark between 2 and 4 A.M. Nonetheless, four young explorers would always remember that evening as one of the longest nights of their lives.

It took only an hour to stow the now disassembled Icehawk and most of Qav and Conor's gear in the Norse house. For security, they buttressed the exterior of the heavy but unhinged door with a considerable pile of rock, using the lowest of the three uncovered windows as entrance and exit. That window, about five feet off the ground, had a rock ledge on the inside that was an ideal sentry post for the rotating guard detail that Jack proposed. They planned to sleep in three-hour shifts until the storm passed.

But first they had to formulate a plan. There were two key questions: First, should they escape together at the first opportunity, or risk capture to save their elderly mentors? Second, what use, if any, should they make of Anaq's rifle?

Jack, still Dansgaard's successor as "leader," tackled the gun issue first. He was greatly disturbed that the option even existed.

"Look, guys, we must get rid of that rifle. Under no circumstance, even if our lives were in mortal danger, would it be justified to use violence against the people who inhabit this valley."

"What if Julia or Conor were attacked? Wouldn't you do whatever was necessary to defend them?" Qav responded.

"No," Jack was steadfast. "I wouldn't use the rifle."

"Not even a warning shot?" Conor asked.

"Look, these people have never seen a rifle before, so a warning shot would not necessarily deter them. Likely you would actually have to wound or kill one of them before they understood the danger. And that is not morally acceptable."

"I agree completely with Jack," Julia piped in. "As scientists we have a special responsibility to minimize the disturbance to this culture. However frightened we might be at the moment, we have to remember that they are the truly endangered ones. We have all the technology and power. They don't."

"I take your point," Qav conceded. "But how then are we going to rescue the old guys?"

"We're not," Jack spoke very quietly. "Any further contact with the locals might be disastrous. I advise that we leave as soon as the storm breaks."

Qav looked disconsolate. "But my grandad . . ."

"I know." Jack was pained. "But we must trust in the instructions left behind by Dansgaard. You and Conor were wrong to have set out on your own."

Julia nodded in agreement as Conor and Qav stared at the floor.

For the next couple of hours, as the wind began to howl ominously outside, the kids distracted themselves in various tasks. Conor took the first sentry turn, while Julia carefully inventoried the supplies left by Anaq and Dansgaard—too much tobacco and not enough chocolate, in her opinion. Qav tinkered with the communications gear in the hope that either his grandfather or Dansgaard would try to send a message. Jack, for his part, double-checked the Icehawk, carefully scrutinizing the wings and frame for any tears or weak points.

Anaq's rifle, meanwhile, had been put out of action. The bolt was placed in one pack and the cartridges in another to prevent any resort to gunfire in an emergency. Jack had wanted to throw the ammunition away, but Qav convinced him that the rifle might be essential in dealing with polar bears on the way back to Tingmiarmiut.

39. TROUBLED SLEEP

"It's ragin' wild outside." Conor had both hands cupped over his eyes trying to peer out the window.

By the time Julia took her turn as sentry, the Norse house was the center of a maelstrom. Everyone but Qav, who had grown up with such things, was appalled by the ferocity of the wind.

"This is an Arctic hurricane," shouted Jack, as he and Conor struggled to secure the Icehawk against the gales that had invaded the house. "Come on, Julia, climb down. There is no danger of attack while this storm is raging."

Wrapping themselves in sleeping bags left by Dansgaard and Anaq, and the windsheet of the tent, the four friends huddled disconsolately in a corner. It was almost impossible to talk because of roar of the wind through the windows. There was such a powerful updraft in the chimney that Julia's little backpack was sucked across the floor and straight up the flue before anyone could react. Julia imagined it soaring into the stratosphere.

Conor finally managed to doze off, followed by Julia, who had burrowed her face into the shoulder of his parka. Qav and Jack remained awake.

Qav looked worried. "Still upset about the rifle?" Jack asked.

"No, I am frightened by this house."

"Yeah, pretty spooky in a storm."

"No, it's more than that. This house is all wrong."

"What do you mean?"

"It's simply too big and cold and badly designed. The ceiling is too high, even for a cattle byre."

Qav was right. "Maybe it was their church?" Jack offered.

"Maybe, or perhaps a trap."

"Trap?" Jack had lost Qav's train of thought. "A trap for whom?"

"For lost idiots like us," Qav shivered.

The wind grew even louder. Soon both Qav and Jack had joined Conor and Julia in troubled, anxious sleep.

Jack had yet another of his odd dreams. He was alone in the Norse house. It was freezing cold but silent. Sunlight, not wind and snow, was pouring into the house. He climbed to the window ledge to look outside. The house was perched on top of an iceberg alone in the middle of a vast ocean.

40. "THEY'RE COMING!"

Dot! Dot, Dot, Dot! Dash! Dot! Dot!

Jack woke up with a start as one of the Garmins came alive. The storm had stopped and it was again light outside.

As the other kids stirred, Jack grabbed the communicator. Someone was signaling in old-fashioned Morse Code. It must be Dansgaard, still unable to talk but using the emergency button on his Garmin.

"What is it?" Julia asked, as everyone gathered around Jack.

"It's the Professor, but be quiet and let me see if I can make out the message." Fortunately, Jack had studied Morse Code as part of his otherwise fruitless application for a license to fly the Icehawk.

Jack turned white.

"My God, Jack, what's up?" asked Conor.

"Dansgaard's message is this: 'They're coming for you! They're coming for you!' The Morse signal abruptly stopped. The four were momentarily frozen in fear, bordering on panic.

Jack regained his composure. "Conor, quick! Scoot up to the window and see what's outside."

His brother didn't hesitate, and Jack tossed him a pair of binoculars. He scanned the valley north of the house. Qav grabbed another pair, and like Spiderman, he used tiny toeholds in the stone to climb to the highest window, which overlooked the back of the house.

"Nothing yet," said Conor gravely. "Ditto," added Qav.

"What should we do?" Julia was worried.

Jack was again his cool, rational self. "There is probably time for

Conor and Qav to reach the cliff face and descend to their kayaks. They should return to base camp and radio for help. Whether we like it or not, we need the outside world to rescue us."

Qav jumped down from his perch. "Wait, Jack, I have another idea."

"What's that?"

"Our best safeguard is the Icehawk, which only you know how to fly. So it would make more sense for you and Julia to hide and let the Halloween guys capture me and Conor."

"Why don't we all hide?" Julia interrupted.

"Because they would search until they found us. But remember, they probably don't suspect that the two of you are here—Clown Face will just say he saw a huge bird in the sky. So if Conor and I give ourselves up, they may not look any further."

"What would be the point?" Julia persisted.

"We can use our Garmins to send you and Jack a homing signal that you can follow in the Icehawk. You'll then be able to tell rescuers exactly where we are being held. Besides, it is safer and faster for you to fly back to Tingmiarmiut than for us to tempt Puisortoq again in our kayaks."

"I suppose that does make more sense." Julia turned to look at Jack.

Jack was about to answer when Conor yelled: "There's something moving, maybe a quarter of a mile away."

The three kids quickly crowded on the ledge next to him. Initially they saw nothing, then there was motion in the willow brush several hundred meters away. A group of figures emerged.

"My god, it's him," gasped Conor. Sure enough, in the lead was the hunter with the grotesque makeup. He was followed by three other men and a boy, none of whom had painted faces. About a hundred yards from the house, they stopped.

For seemingly endless minutes the group stood glaring at the house. Conor pushed everyone else away from the window and out of sight, exposing himself brazenly. He had decided to stare down the painted man, so he crossed his arms and looked ahead defiantly.

Julia pulled at his leg. "Conor, at this point we have nothing to lose by being friendly," she implored.

Conor smiled down at her. He then hoisted himself out of the window as far as possible. Waving at the mystery people, he shouted:

"Hi, there! Top of the mornin'! Nice day, isn't it! Coming in for your cup of tea?"

Qav, as scared as he was, couldn't hide his wonderment at his boldness. "Conor, you maniac!"

But Conor's nonchalant pleasantries terrified the locals, who retreated back to the edge of the dwarf willow. The painted man turned around and yelled something in a strange high-pitched dialect of Norse, seemingly appealing for help.

Suddenly something else emerged from the brush. Conor would recall it afterwards as the most extraordinary sight of the entire adventure.

A figure who looked like a ghostly monk clad in a dark cassock was mounted on a bull mammoth. The mammoth—the patriarch of the herd, as Conor would later learn—had magnificent helical-shaped tusks perhaps six feet in length. The rider, his face hidden by a hood, was carrying a long, rune-engraved stave. He was followed by another half-dozen hunters.

Conor was amazed but undaunted. He swung out on the ledge, his feet dangling down. His body screened the other kids while they peered out.

"I think we're about to meet the Wizard of Oz," Conor whispered to his mates. "What do we do now?"

"Hurry, Jack and Julia, scramble down and hide in the chimney." Qav was thinking quickly.

Julia grabbed Jack by the arm. Jack looked at Conor.

"Go for it, big brother. You can rescue us later. Don't worry, they won't eat us."

Jack wasn't so sure, but he conceded that Qav's plan made sense. "OK, but be sure to hide your Garmins as carefully as you can and keep the homing signals on. We'll follow behind in the Icehawk. I'm not leaving you here."

Conor smiled. "Hurry, they're coming now."

The chimney had a huge hearth, big enough to stand up inside. Qav gave Julia, then Jack, a shoulder lift. Inside there were plenty of small rock ledges. Julia climbed up about six feet and wedged herself tightly. Jack was just below. Qav checked to see if they were visible from below.

"Quick, climb higher, I can still see you." Julia wriggled up into the very top of the dirty chimney with Jack behind her. Jack then fixed a nylon haul line as Qav and Conor gingerly maneuvered the disassembled Icehawk vertically into the chimney. They were barely able to fit it inside without damaging it. Jack then hoisted it out of view.

Conor whispered, "See ya later, bro."

Jack and Julia waited in suspense.

After a few minutes, they heard commotion below. Jack bit his lip. The noise, which lasted for about ten minutes, gave way to silence. Jack and Julia waited a few minutes more in their cramped space, then Julia—an experienced gymnast—gingerly climbed out the top of the chimney. "All clear," she whispered down to Jack. She then scrambled down to the ground.

The door of the house had been pried off, perhaps by the trunk of a trained mammoth. All of their gear was gone. Indeed, there was no evidence that anyone had ever been there.

"Hurry, Julia." With some difficulty, Julia assisted from below as Jack lowered the Icehawk. A strut broke as they pulled it out of the chimney, but it was otherwise undamaged. It took Jack about fifteen minutes to reassemble it for flight.

Julia meanwhile monitored her Garmin. The homing signal from Qav and Conor was coming in clearly. On her little screen, she watched the pinpoint of light that represented the captives as they headed up the valley. Then the light stopped moving. They had arrived at the hot springs.

EPISODE SEVEN: *An Artic Pitcairn*

Ela. It would be best if no one went down there to discover them.
They may be happy, they may be sad, but it would be best if they
were left alone. Left alone to live or starve as they choose.
Attuniannaguk! Best not to touch them at all . . .

The hunter Avannag talking about a rumored secret
culture living on the southeast Greenland coast. [15]

*B*eing captured was a different experience than either Qav or Conor had imagined. When their besiegers finally pulled away the door, the boys had expected to come face to face with fierce, angry warriors. In fact, their captors—all but one, that is—were mild-mannered and friendly.

Most astonishing was Clown Face. He was actually a man of middle age, with the mixed Inuit and Norse features so characteristic of Greenlanders in general. Despite his strange facepaint, his manner was gentle and reassuring. Like a long-lost uncle, he patted each boy affectionately on the shoulder while the others smiled and chattered.

Then he pointed to the door and spoke in short, friendly syllables. Conor turned to Qav to see if he understood what was being said.

"He says, 'please come, come,' and he also calls us 'sons.' Shall we oblige him?"

"Sure, let's follow the yellow brick road."

Qav tried a few words of Danish. The painted man seemed to be struggling with the meaning, so Qav switched to his limited knowledge of Icelandic, the language closest to the Old Norse of the Greenlanders. Rapport was instant.

"*Ja, Ja! Skal!*" Clown Face warmly grasped Qav's hands and began to jabber.

Qav didn't understand all of it, but thought he got the gist.

"He says we are kin. People of the North. Vikings," Qav whispered to Conor.

"What's his name?"

"Bjarni, son of Tor."

"Greetings, Bjarni." Conor boldly stuck out his hand. Again it was gratefully embraced.

Smiling, Bjarni pointed to the door. Qav, in turn, pointed to their gear. Bjarni nodded and gave an order. The other hunters began to gather up the backpacks and boxes. Qav and Conor anxiously glanced back at the fireplace where Jack and Julia were hiding, then followed Bjarni outside.

They immediately found themselves looking at some very hairy knees. Although only half the height of its forebears, the father mammoth was nonetheless impressive. He was seven or eight feet tall at the shoulder, and Conor estimated he probably weighed about three tons. He had a dark-brown wooly coat, a shoulder hump, and a sloping back. The ears on his magnificently domed head were small and surprisingly humanlike, an adaptation to the extreme cold. His jaws contained the massive molars—grindstones, almost—that processed the two hundred pounds of clubmoss, grass, dwarf birch, and arctic sagebrush that were the required daily diet of a mature mammoth.

Sitting on his back was the altogether less friendly figure in the hooded cassock. His face was angular, with a hawklike nose and piercing black eyes; on his chin were wisps of a white beard. He looked rather like an ancient Chinese emperor.

Qav tried a friendly greeting in Icelandic. He did not get a response.

The mammoth, however, unfurled its trunk in the direction of the boys. Conor brazenly walked up and gently petted it. The great beast emitted a low pitched reverberation that almost sounded like purring. Conor smiled, but the animal's rider glared and said something to Bjarni, who gently pulled Conor away.

Bjarni said something that he underscored by vigorously shaking his head back and forth. Qav started to translate but was interrupted by the rider himself. It was a short rant that made Qav frown.

"I'm not sure I understood all of it, but his name is Halldor. He is the *galdramaour.*"

"What's that?" Conor was wide-eyed.

"The sorcerer or wizard. In medieval Greenland and Iceland, black magic, called *galdur,* existed side by side with Christianity . . ."[16]

Halldor, impatient, barked a new order. Qav responded with an insolent look.

"Our wizard orders us to move on and reminds you not to touch his mammoth again."

Halldor whispered something to the great beast and it promptly turned around and started back up the valley. Everyone else followed in an irregular column. Bjarni put his arm around Qav and spoke softly to him. Qav nodded, then turned toward Conor.

"Bjarni says not to worry. Everyone is happy that Halldor's magic brought us here. In fact, he claims that they have been dreaming about us for a long time. We are the 'new sons.'"

"That sounds a bit spooky, but ask him about the old guys."

Qav relayed the question to Bjarni, who instantly became nervous. He stuttered a reply and averted his eyes.

"He says we will see our 'grandfathers' shortly. But he is not allowed to say more."

"You know, Qav," Conor furrowed his brows, "we may be the celebrities of the hour, but I fear Halldor has sinister plans for Anaq and Dansgaard. We need to talk to Jack as soon as possible."

Qav looked depressed. "Perhaps I shouldn't have let your brother talk me into disabling the rifle."

42. ADOPTION AND ANXIETY

While Jack put the Icehawk back together, Julia watched from the roof with binoculars.

"They're almost out of sight," she told Jack.

He pulled his Garmin from its holster and checked to see if the homing signal was still being transmitted. "The signal is strong. Better come down and give me a hand."

As Julia began to shimmy down the side of the house, she noticed something in the brush behind the house. It was the little backpack that had blown up the chimney.

"Look, Jack, some good luck. The jetstream didn't get my backpack after all."

Jack smiled. "What's in it?"

Julia looked embarrassed. "Nothing very important . . ."

"Oh, come on, Julia, if it wasn't so important, why did you insist on bringing it?"

Now Julia was starting to get mad. "Well, take a look for yourself."

Jack opened the pack and dumped its contents on a wing of the Icehawk. "Hmm, let's see . . . two pairs of long underwear, pajamas, a scarf, a toothbrush, dental floss, and a box of . . . What is this? . . . yes, laundry powder." He laughed. "Cleanliness, I suppose, is next to godliness.

Especially when you're lost in the Ice Age."

"Shall I leave it here?" Julia was blushing.

"No, it doesn't weigh much, and if worse comes to worst, you might have to wash all the Vikings' dirty underwear." He chuckled.

Julia hit Jack hard on the shoulder, then lifted her hand to hit him again.

"Ouch. OK, you're even."

Julia's hand was still in the air when both of their Garmins started to beep.

They grabbed for their communicators like two gunfighters in the Old West trying to beat each other to the draw. Julia was quickest. It was Conor.

"Julia, turn on your screen. Do you see our position?"

"Yes, very clear, you're near the hot springs. Is this their camp?"

"Yeah, I think it's actually a permanent village."

"Are you in danger?"

"No, we're fine. Old Clown Face is actually a good guy, as are most of the others. They seemed to have adopted us, permanently."

"For godsakes, Conor, what does 'permanently' mean?" Jack interrupted. "And how do you know what their intentions are? Can Qav talk to them?"

"Yeah, Qav is chatting up a storm in his broken Icelandic. The locals are led by a rather unpleasant wizard named Halldor."

"A wizard?" Julia sounded amazed.

"Yes, a 'galdramoor,' or something like that. Qav says magic was part of the Old Norse culture."

Jack again interrupted. "What about the old guys?"

"We should find out shortly. But I'm worried that Halldor is planning something sinister.

"Wait a second." Jack was agitated. "I thought you said you were in no danger?"

"No, we're not. In fact, we're the center of attention, the new kids on the block. But Anaq and Dansgaard may be in peril. They're being held as Halldor's prisoners."

"Well, what should we do next?"

"You and Julia stay put for awhile. Let Qav and me see if we can find out what Halldor is up to. We'll try to get back to you within a few hours. Be patient."

"OK, we'll hold here for awhile. But I'm warning you, Conor, if for any reason we haven't heard from you in four hours, we're airborne and on our way."

"That's reasonable." Conor was doing his best to soothe his brother. "So over and out . . ."

"Hang on for a second." Jack had an idea. "Look, do you remember the Morse code SOS signal?"

"Sure, everyone knows that."

"Well, in an emergency, if you can't talk to me, tap it out on the Garmin. Got that?"

"Roger."

"OK, roger yourself. And keep some of that mammoth stew for us. Julia and I are famished." Jack put the Garmin back in its holster. He looked at Julia with an expression that combined frustration and anxiety.

"Don't worry, Jack, they're safe and sound for the time being. And look what treasures I found in the backpack that you made so much fun of." Julia held up a pair of energy bars.

Jack instantly brightened. "Yum."

43. A WARM WELCOME

After a few miles' walk across the mammoth steppe, the column came to a wall of steam. Halldor and his mammoth suddenly vanished, and a minute later Conor lost sight of Qav although he was only a few feet away. A hand—it was Bjarni's—steadied Conor. He felt like he was walking straight into the strangest dream.

After a hundred yards or so, the curtain of warm fog opened to reveal a truly astounding oasis of terraced hot springs, sulfur fumaroles, boiling streams, and waterfalls.

Conor looked puzzled. "I didn't know so much geothermal activity was possible in Greenland."

"Well, there are the famous hot springs in Uunartoq on the south-west coast," Qav responded, "but you are right, this is amazing. Perhaps it is a relic of the North Atlantic hot spot."

Qav explained to Conor that a million years ago—just yesterday in geological time—this part of Greenland had passed over a stationary "hot spot," a blowtorch-like plume of superheated rock originating in the Earth's mantle. Subsequent plate-tectonic movement shifted what became Iceland over the hot spot, where it is still creating new volcanoes.

"Yeah, I'm sure you're right. So this is the last ember of an old flame."

"Look, Conor, can you believe this?" Ahead was a considerable village of turf-and-rock cottages. They were all much lower to the ground and better insulated than the Norse edifice at the head of the valley. A network of ditches carried hot water inside the structures.

"What an ingenious heating system!" Qav was impressed.

"Look to your left." Conor pointed beyond the cluster of homes to a series of fields with high rock walls in the distance.

"My god, cattle!" To a native East Greenlander like Qav this was an even stranger and more improbable occurrence than living mammoths.

Bjarni, amused by Qav's excitement, spoke to him.

"Bjarni says that they grow much hay and have many milk cows, but the something-or-others—I think he means the mammoths—frequently knock down the walls and trample the fields."

"How about people? Is this the only village?"

Qav translated. "Bjarni says this is the only 'people home.' The other valleys are sacred grazing range for the mammoths."

Bjarni pointed to a low ridge in the background.

"He says that just beyond that ridge is the village of the spirits." Qav interrogated Bjarni for a moment. "There is something called the 'house of sleep' and also a great 'water oracle.' Halldor lives there."

"Ask him if that's where Halldor is holding the old guys."

Qav started to question Bjarni, but there was shouting and commotion in the distance. A mob of people, all dressed in skins, were running toward them.

"Are we in trouble?" Qav nervously asked Bjarni in Icelandic.

Bjarni laughed.

A minute later, the two boys were surrounded by the shy but smiling faces of several dozen women and children. A group of men and boys stood apart, but their expressions also seemed friendly. Halldor, mysteriously, was nowhere to be seen.

Conor's failure to respond to their queries initially puzzled the locals, but Qav explained that he couldn't speak Norse. To the boys' amazement, a middle-aged woman with stronger Inuit features than the others addressed Conor in Greenlandic. The others winced and looked embarrassed, as if speaking Greenlandic were generally prohibited.

Qav replied that Conor couldn't speak the Inuit tongue either. Someone made a sympathetic gesture that indicated he must be a deaf mute.

"For godsakes, Qav, tell them I am not a space alien." Conor's strange-sounding words caused immediate consternation.

Qav spoke at some length, although he frequently had to resort to Danish or Greenlandic for names and concepts he lacked in Icelandic. Everyone listened patiently but obviously without clear comprehension. The idea of people other than Vikings or "Straelings"—as the Norse derisively called the Inuit—seemed to be entirely outside the local mental universe.

Finally Qav gave up. "Sorry, Conor, I've tried everything, but they don't understand. For the present, you'll simply have to live with the identity of a funny-looking Norseman with an acute speech disability."

Conor frowned, but his spirits were lifted by the giggling children. A woman motioned to them to come into her home. "Chow time?" Conor asked Qav.

"You got it." Qav was as hungry as a polar wolf.

There was only room for a dozen or so people in the low turf house (which reminded Conor of a crofter's cottage in the west of Ireland), but the rest of the community gathered expectantly outside the door.

The family dinner table was ingeniously constructed of thick mammoth hide with juvenile tusks as legs. It was very similar, Conor thought, to what you might find in the traditional home of a Kenyan notable.

The very welcome meal, meanwhile, was served in soapstone dishes similar to those used by the pre-contact Inuit as well as, surprisingly, some cheap modern plastic plates.

The generous cuisine consisted of turnips, barley, wild greens, crowberries, and a fatty stew with a pungent taste that was probably aged mammoth. Sour milk—the Norse staple—was served to Conor in a gorgeous silver chalice of Viking design and to Qav in a styrofoam cup.

Qav interrogated his hosts about the plastic plates and cup. One of them went to the back of the house and returned with a fiberglass fragment of a canoe or kayak.

"They climb down the cliffs every summer to beachcomb and gather seaweed; it is one of their most important subsistence activities. But they don't have a clue where this stuff actually comes from. They think Halldor's magic summons it from the sea and air."

Conor grimaced. "This Halldor is a world-class huckster." Qav nodded.

To the delight of their hosts, Qav and Conor dug into dinner with great gusto. While they ate, each member of the family shyly approached the boys and touched their hair or patted them on the shoulder. It was a moving demonstration of affection. Outside, the other locals began singing a soft song, almost like a lullabye.

Conor wondered to himself, "How could such gentle folk allow themselves to be ruled by such a dark force as Halldor?"

44. RELIEF

Qav explained to his hosts that he had to relieve himself, and he was promptly shown to a ditch behind the cattle byre. A small crowd gathered to watch. Qav, squatting, begged for some privacy. They giggled at his unexpected modesty but obediently left him alone.

As soon as they had gone, he reached inside his anorak and took the Garmin out of the holster. "Jack, Julia, can you read me?"

"Roger." It was Jack this time. Are you OK?"

"Fine. They just gave us a big feed. The welcoming committee is very sweet. Hard to believe that we were so scared of them just a few hours ago."

"How about Halldor?"

"He has a separate encampment where the old guys are being held. There's some kind of ceremonial center there. It sounds slightly sinister."

"Should we come now?"

"No, please, sit tight until tomorrow. Let us try to meet with Halldor and check out the situation with my grandfather and Dansgaard. We'll call back as soon as we can."

Silence. Jack was tired, frustrated, and still worried that Qav and Conor were in more danger than they realized. On the other hand, it was probably foolish to drop out of the sky until more was known about the fate of Dansgaard and Anaq.

"OK, I suppose you're right. But keep a very close rein on my brother. Conor is too impetuous."

"OK. Sorry, we can't share our mammoth stew with you. It's quite good, actually."

"Don't worry, Julia dug up some energy bars. If we get too hungry we'll start gnawing on our boots. But be careful—promise?"

"Absolutely. Over and out."

45. HALLDOR'S SPELL

The boys' fatigue was obvious to their hosts, so despite the community's intense curiosity about their newly adopted sons, Qav and Conor were allowed to doze off in a corner of the house. When their eyes were firmly closed, one of the older girls gently covered each of them with a warm polar bear pelt.

The next day, bright and clear as any that summer, energized Qav and Conor.

"What a gorgeous day! Hard to believe we're the prisoners of ancient Vikings, isn't it?" Qav grinned at Conor.

Conor looked at the kind faces of his hosts, and then, through the window, at the group of kids gathered outside. "No, this isn't a bad prison at all."

Bjarni joined them for a breakfast of berries and sour milk.

Qav repeated the request to see their grandfathers. Bjarni seemed less nervous about the subject than the day before.

"Yes, Bjarni says he will take us to Halldor. The old guys are with him."

Most of the village followed them to top of the ridge, but everyone stopped there. Bjarni spoke a few words to his neighbors and then whispered something to Qav.

"He says Halldor has ordered us to proceed on our own. He apologizes that he can't come with us but says not to worry."

Conor frowned. "OK, let's give it a go. But I don't understand how a whole community can be so intimidated by one man, even if he is a sorcerer."

It took the boys about twenty minutes to cross the valley to Halldor's camp. As they came closer, they realized what an extraordinary place it really was. Halldor's house—an imposing circular structure of rock and turf—was a few hundred yards away from a sulfur-stained, steaming mound that Qav, who visited Iceland frequently with his parents, instantly recognized as a geyser.

More amazingly, directly in front of Halldor's door was an aircraft wing stuck vertically into the ground like a totem pole. It was steel gray with a red-and-white star symbol. Qav looked at Conor for an explanation.

"Jack's the expert on aircraft, but I think it's the wing of a P-38 Lightning, an American fighter from World War II. Hundreds were ferried across Greenland to England. This must be from an old crash on the Inland Ice."

Halldor emerged from behind the totem wing and motioned to them to stop. He spoke to Qav in a voice that was somber but less unfriendly than yesterday.

"Halldor welcomes us. He says that we are the future of his people. He promises to be our teacher."

"That's jolly good, but ask him where our 'grandfathers' are."

Qav repeated the question. Halldor, surprisingly, nodded his head, smiled, and invited the boys to come inside.

The interior was divided by an interior wall made of stone and wattle and covered with bear pelts. The room they were standing in was a eclectic museum of wonders ranging from a bronze ship's compass ("Where did he get that?") to the painted skull of a walrus. In one corner was all the gear from the Norse house. Halldor walked over and picked out the two objects that obviously most intrigued him: a video camera and Anaq's boltless rifle.

"Halldor want us to explain how their magic works."

Conor had a hunch that one of the old guys had probably managed to film part of their capture. He turned on the viewing screen of the video, and as he suspected, footage immediately appeared of Halldor's band breaking into the house. He showed the image to Halldor.

The great sorcerer fell back on the floor as if struck by a bolt of lightning. There was a heartbreaking expression of terror on his face, and, for a fleeting moment, Conor felt guilty for tricking him. Then he remembered why they were there.

"OK, tell Halldor that this is the kind of magic that we bring, powers beyond his wildest dreams. We want to see the old guys now." Conor struck a defiant pose.

Qav translated. Halldor slowly regained his composure, although he was still too frightened to get near Conor or his magical box. He pointed to a crude door made from a ship's plank similar to that used for the door at the Norse house.

Conor pushed the door open. It was so dark inside that he initially couldn't see anything. Then as his eyes began to adjust, he saw two forms, dead or asleep, on the floor. Their faces were painted in the same grotesque design as Bjarni's.

Qav rushed over and tried to awake Anaq. He didn't stir, but when Qav put his face close to his grandfather's he could feel his warm breath. He then checked on Dansgaard.

"They're alive but in some kind of coma or trance." Qav, angry, started yelling at Halldor.

Halldor opened his cape and produced an antique tincture bottle. Halldor walked over to his prone captives and bent down. He opened the bottle and passed it under Anaq's nostrils, then Dansgaard's.

"What's he doing?" asked Conor.

"I think he's trying to wake them from his spell," said Qav, still upset.

"He says he will be back in a short while. He's going to the stream to fetch water." Qav frowned. "But I don't trust him."

"Of course not," replied Conor. "But for the moment we have the more powerful magic."

Anaq, the first to sit up, began rubbing his eyes. Qav ran over and hugged him. Then Dansgaard, a little groggier, also began to regain his bearings.

"Conor, my god, you are here. Where are Jack and Julia? Are they at base camp?"

"No, they're waiting at the Norse house for our report. They brought the Icehawk."

Dansgaard looked horrified. He translated for Anaq, who shook his head gravely.

"I thought Jack was responsible. He completely disobeyed my orders . . ."

Conor interrupted. "No, Professor, it wasn't his fault. Qav and I came here in our kayaks. He had no choice."

Dansgaard was unmollified but he changed the subject.

"Do any of you have a runny nose or a cough? Any symptoms of a cold or flu?"

"No," Qav answered this time, "why do you ask?"

"Because we pose a deadly danger to these poor people. They have no immunity to our most common diseases. They could all die in a few weeks if we aren't extraordinarily careful."

Conor and Qav nodded, ashamed they hadn't thought of the infection risk.

Anaq went to find something to rub the paint off his face, but Dansgaard continued his interrogation.

"How about old people? Did you see any old people in the village?"

The boys were surprised by the question.

Qav looked at Conor. "No, now that you mention it, we didn't see any elders apart from Halldor himself. What does this imply, Professor?"

Dansgaard got up and walked to the door. He looked outside to see if Halldor was eavesdropping. Satisfied that the sorcerer was gone, he turned to the boys.

"Have either of you ever heard of Pitcairn Island?"

"What does that have to do with the missing old people?" Qav was impatient.

"Calm down, Qav," Dansgaard patted his shoulder. "You'll see the connection in a moment."

"Pitcairn," Conor responded, "is a tiny island somewhere in the Eastern Pacific. Jack and I used to collect its stamps. It was originally settled, I think by eighteenth-century British mutineers. It's a famous story. The leader of the mutineers was Fletcher Christian. But I can't remember the name of the ship."

"*Bounty, Mutiny on the Bounty.*" Qav had seen both movie versions of the story. "But so what?"

"Indulge me, Qav." Dansgaard patted his shoulder. "After setting Captain Bligh adrift, Fletcher Christian sailed the *Bounty* in search of an island so remote that the Royal Navy would never find it. Eventually the mutineers and their Tahitian wives discovered Pitcairn. Today, two centuries later, fifty of their descendants still live there."

"Their genes must be in a twist with so much intermarriage in so small a population. Funny, I've just been reading a book, *The Island of the Colorblind,* that talks about this subject." Connor was referring to his favorite science writer, Oliver Sacks, and his best-selling account of isolated oceanic societies.

"That's exactly the point." Dansgaard was very pleased. "Very soon after settlement, the *Bounty* survivors fell out and began fighting each other. Only one mutineer survived, along with a small number of women and children.

"So the Pitcairners' heredity has this incredible bottleneck. With constant interbreeding, it ensures an extreme risk of inheritable illness and disability. The Pitcairners' only solution is to marry outsiders and diversify their gene pool. Otherwise they would eventually become extinct."

Qav suddenly understood. "I think you're suggesting, Doctor, that the Lost Vikings are caught in the same biological bind as the Pitcairn population."

Conor finished the thought. "And somehow they've managed to figure out that the survival of their community depends upon incorporating outsiders. That might explain why we met a woman who was obviously a Greenlander."

"It would also explain why we're so popular," Qav piped in. Both boys chuckled at the thought of being prime breeding stock for future generations of mammoth hunters.

"Very good. But this is only one half of the Vikings' dilemma. What is their other fundamental ecological problem?" Dansgaard was playing schoolteacher.

"Carrying capacity, obviously." Conor was still trying to work through in his mind the complex algebra of balancing vegetation supply, mammoth population, and human subsistence.

"Indeed," said Dansgaard. "Now what mechanism do you suppose this culture has evolved to ensure that population is regularly equilibrated to the resource base?"

"First of all, tell us how this plays out on Pitcairn?" Qav asked.

"Pitcairn, I am afraid, is too small to be self-sufficient," Dansgaard responded. "The population has repeatedly outgrown the available food supply. When the *Bounty* crew arrived they found the ruins of a much older Polynesian settlement. Presumably the Polynesians either died off from famine or were forced to evacuate the island."

"So how did the mutineers cope?" Conor was puzzled.

"The modern Pitcairners have avoided catastrophe by sending their surplus populations to Norfolk Island—a larger, more sustainable environment—or to New Zealand. And, apparently they also make a living selling postage stamps to Conor and Jack."

The boys laughed.

Dansgaard continued. "The Valley of the Runes, of course, doesn't issue postage stamps with handsome images of pygmy mammoths, and hopefully never will. But it does share Pitcairn's dilemma of fixed resources and a growing population. Although this is a much larger ecosystem, at some point in the last six hundred years population growth would have created a susbistence crisis or led to the overhunting of the mammoths."

He paused for dramatic effect. "So what ingenious mechanism do you think these Vikings have evolved to adjust the population to carrying capacity?"

The boys were stumped for a minute. Then the same idea lit up lightbulbs in Qav's and Conor's skulls simultaneously. Their jaws dropped.

"Oh my god. They cull the elderly." Conor was horrified.

"I knew Halldor was a murderer," added Qav.

"Halldor did not invent this custom," corrected Dansgaard. "He's merely the custodian of tradition. Better to sacrifice the seniors than let babies starve. From what I can gather, the locals imagine that their grandparents are simply being sent into a blissful sleep."

"By the sedatives that Halldor gave you and Anaq?" asked Conor.

"No, not nearly potent enough. As best Anaq and I can figure, that stone structure that you may have noticed at the base of the geyser is an entrance to a underground chamber. Enough carbon dioxide or methane probably seeps into it to do the trick in a few minutes."

"A gas chamber?" Qav was white-faced.

"Yes and no. In their belief system it is merely a place of gentle sleep. More than likely, no violence is involved. The elderly probably go gladly to their good night. Then they are spirited away, somewhere over the mountain, to a great ice cave on the flank of Puisortoq. This is their Valhalla, where the ancestors are supposed to live forever. I'd very much like to visit it. But not by the method Halldor intends." Dansgaard chuckled.

Qav asked, "So what's the escape plan, Doctor? We need to organize quickly before Halldor returns."

Dansgaard never had a chance to answer.

EPISODE EIGHT: *Sorcerers' Duel*

47. A PERMANENT VACATION

*H*alldor was outside, mounted on his mammoth. He had marshalled a posse of all the men in the village. Some carried ropes made of strips of mammoth hide, while others carried staves.

The *galdramaour* barked an order, and Bjarni and several of the larger men dutifully entered the house.

Anaq blocked their path. He wore a warlike expression that unsettled the Vikings, who immediately backed off.

Dansgaard, his face still painted in the same pattern as Bjarni's, put his hand on Anaq's shoulder, then whispered in his ear. Anaq shook his head. Dansgaard whispered again. Anaq gave his old friend a long look, then turned and sat down in the corner.

The Vikings seemed greatly relieved.

Dansgaard spoke to Bjarni while Qav translated for his grandfather.

The gist of the conversation was that Dansgaard apologized to Bjarni for the disruption they had caused and assured him they had not come as enemies. Bjarni replied that, far from foes, they considered them revered kinsmen.

Dansgaard then asked Bjarni what Halldor's intentions were. He replied that the boys, who obviously were so well advanced in the magic arts, would be trained by Halldor as his successors so that Halldor, at last, might be allowed to sleep.

"And us?" Dansgaard asked. Bjarni gently touched the Professor's arm. He explained that it was time for the grandfathers to sleep in the cave of the ancestors. Pointing to the painted design on his own face, he promised that he himself would follow in a few months. Bjarni's demeanor was that of a friendly travel agent offering a permanent vacation in paradise.

Neither Dansgaard or Anaq seemed unduly perturbed, but Qav was panicky. "Conor, quick, they're planning to kill the old guys. Help me assemble the gun."

Qav grabbed the rifle in one hand and began to rummage frantically through the backpacks. Conor helped him, and they soon found the ammunition. In another pack Qav found the bolt.

Dansgaard said something to Anaq, who then placed Qav's left arm in a viselike grip.

"What are you doing?" Dansgaard asked Qav, who was on the verge of tears. "Qav, put the rifle down. There can be no violence here."

"But they are going to kill the two of you."

"That's not how they see it," Dansgaard replied firmly.

With a huge effort Qav broke free of his grandfather's grip and ran into the back room, with Conor following. Within a few seconds they had put the bolt back into rifle and chambered a round. Qav looked at Conor.

"Whatever it takes, Qav, I'm with you."

The Vikings had started to follow the boys, but Dansgaard said something stern to Bjarni, who stopped the others.

The boys reappeared with the rifle.

Now it was Anaq's turn to talk to Qav. His tone was firm but not harsh, as he lectured Qav for seemingly endless minutes. He put his hand on the rifle. Qav, tears streaming down his face, reluctantly yielded it. Anaq took the bolt and cartridge out, then threw the rifle down. He hugged his grandson.

Dansgaard, meanwhile, was whispering to Conor. "Don't try to save us. Return to the village and warn Jack. Escape at the first opportunity. And don't tell anyone in the world about these people or our fate. Do you understand? However difficult, this is your moral and scientific duty."

Conor grimly nodded, then looked at Qav, who seemed absolutely crushed. This was not the way their great adventure was supposed to turn out. Then he remembered the Garmin in its shoulder holster.

Turning sideways to the Vikings, he slipped it out and held it behind his back. Clumsily at first, but then with a steady rhythm, he began to tap out the Morse code SOS signal.

"Come on, Jack," he said quietly to himself. "Swoop down out of the sky and scare the pants off of Halldor."

48. DIVE BOMBER

Jack and Julia sat by the Icehawk and stared hungrily at their boots. The energy bars were long gone, and it had been almost two days since their last real meal.

Julia managed a smile. "What are you thinking, Jack?"

"Wishing I could call out for a pizza. Double cheese with pepperoni and mushrooms."

"Me too. I'm famished."

Suddenly, both their Garmins started to click "Dot-dot—dash—dot-dot."

Julia shouted in to her communicator. "Conor, Qav, come in, come in!"

"They won't answer, Julia. This is the signal, remember, in an emergency where they can't talk. I must get the Icehawk aloft."

Jack climbed into the Icehawk's front seat. "Julia, get out of the way."

Julia stood directly in front of the little plane with her arms folded across her chest.

"Are you kidding?" She glared at Jack.

There was no time for argument, so Jack surrendered. "Then hurry up." Julia quickly buckled herself in and put on her helmet.

Jack throttled the little engine into a high-pitched frenzy and took off in the direction of the sea. When they reached the cliff edge Julia wasn't sure whether their wheels had yet left the ground or not. For a few seconds all she saw was the sea far below, then the Icehawk was again soaring.

Jack turned around to see if Julia was alright.

"Hang on." Jack turned the little plane into a broad bank, circling back over the cliff edge and up the valley. He headed straight for the cloud of steam that marked the edge of the thermal meadow.

For a brief moment they were blinded by the fog. As it began to clear, they saw the village several hundred feet below. It looked abandoned; Jack circled lower for a closer look but didn't see a single soul.

"They must all be at Halldor's compound," he shouted back to Julia.

Two minutes later they had crested a ridge and were in sight of the ceremonial complex, where the entire Viking population had gathered.

"Let's make a dramatic entrance." Jack put the Icehawk into a steep dive toward the throng below. He soon recognized Halldor on the mammoth, and he aimed the nose of the Icehawk straight at him.

The boys' hands were tied behind their backs. Halldor glared at them, but Bjarni was desperately apologetic. He kept whispering reassurances about the boys' bright future as the people's new sorcerers, but Qav was too angry to respond.

Dansgaard and Anaq, whose hands were not bound, were resigned to their fate. Dansgaard believed that it would put the kids, as well as the innocent villagers, in danger if they resisted, but he pleaded with the Vikings to postpone Anaq's "slumber" so that he could continue to teach his skills to the boys.

Dansgaard's speech disconcerted the crowd. There was confused discussion—apparently no one had ever balked at the edge of the Big Sleep before.

Halldor cut the debate short. Reminding his kin that eternal sleep was the goal of life and the reward for all its sufferings, he refused to make any exceptions. Sleep was a gift that he himself yearned for and hoped to enjoy once Qav and Conor had been thoroughly initiated into *galdar*, the shamanic power.

Halldor ordered the ceremony to begin, and a trio of men began to hammer a weird percussion on hollow mammoth bones. A young woman moaned into a baby mammoth's skull, producing an incomparably strange resonance.[17]

Meanwhile, an older woman repainted Anaq's face. The old hunter remained stoic.

Young girls brought garlands of wildflowers for the old men. This amused Dansgaard, who recognized it as an ancient Viking custom. "Amazing," he thought to himself, "the old Norse burial rituals have survived half a millennium of Christianity on the west coast of Greenland and another five hundred years of wizardry here."

A group of villagers opened the gate to the underground chamber, and several went in; they emerged a minute later, coughing loudly.

As Qav and Conor watched in dismay, the young girls began chanting as they solemnly escorted Dansgaard and Anaq to the doorway of the chamber. The crowd pressed forward.

Halldor started to speak, and everyone knelt. The speech, though rather long-winded, was a poetic description of the pleasures that the sleepers would soon enjoy. Some of the villagers were almost in a trance.

Qav whispered desperately to Conor. "When will Jack get here?"

Conor tried not to show his own panic. "Any minute, Qav, just hang on."

But time seemed to have run out. Halldor pointed his staff at Dansgaard and Anaq and spoke an unintelligible incantation. The girls, their faces shining, led the two men into the chamber.

Conor worried for a second that Vikings sacrificed maidens as well, but the girls soon reemerged. The crowd was silent.

Qav's heart was broken. Straining against the ropes that bound his arms, he shouted: "No!"

Seemingly in response, a woman screamed, then another. Suddenly the entire crowd was shouting. Some fell to their knees and covered their eyes, while others ran for their lives.

Conor looked up. The Icehawk was in a steep Stuka-like dive. It truly looked like a vengeful raptor ready to devour Halldor.

The poor *galdramaour*, his mouth gaping, appeared petrified inside his hooded cassock, too terrified to move.

Conor was afraid that Jack was going to decapitate Halldor. Indeed, he swept so close that if Halldor had been wearing a top hat, the wing of the Icehawk would have sliced it in half.

As Jack soared up and began to circle back, Conor broke out of his reverie. "Quick, Qav, see if you can work free of your ropes!" Both boys struggled desperately while Bjarni and the other Vikings were distracted by fear.

Conor, a bit skinnier than Qav, managed to free his hands first. He bent over and quickly untied the loose rope that shackled his ankles, then sprinted for the underground chamber without waiting for Qav who, nonetheless, followed behind, hopping like a mad rabbit since his legs and arms were still tied.

With enough adrenaline flowing through his muscles to make Superman dizzy, Conor ripped opened the door and bolted down a short flight of stone stairs. He found Dansgaard lying unconscious, but Anaq was still awake.

"Jack's here! Come on, let's get the Professor out!" Conor had forgotten that Anaq didn't speak English, but the old hunter was already in action. With some difficulty, they dragged Dansgaard up the stairs and into the cool clear light. Qav came hopping toward them.

Just then Jack set the Icehawk down between the chamber and the crowd. He quickly unbuckled himself and Julia. They emerged from the Icehawk like young gods sent from the sun.

50. THE CHALLENGE

Halldor and his mammoth had fled, and the remaining Vikings were still in shock. For ten or fifteen minutes, there was a stalemate of awestruck silence.

Qav and Anaq worked frantically to revive Dansgaard. Qav performed mouth-to-mouth resuscitation as his grandfather pumped the Professor's chest. Finally, coughing and choking, he came back to life.

"That's the second time today you have awakened me from a sound sleep," he chided Qav, in a hoarse voice. Qav, his ankles still tied together, laughed in relief.

Meanwhile, the other kids were facing down the Vikings. Jack nervously held hands with Julia and Conor, not knowing what might happen next.

Finally, the woman with the kind face who had been Qav and Conor's hostess the previous evening came forward. She fell down on her knees in front of Jack and started a terrible and inscrutable lamentation. Others soon followed, until almost half the village was tearing its hair and wailing. The kids were flabbergasted.

Dansgaard, supported by Qav and Anaq, walked up behind Jack.

"Well, Jack, do you see what your Indiana Jones stunt has accomplished?"

"What's happening?" Jack asked anxiously.

"They're anointing you their new deity, a superwizard at least, perhaps a sky god."

Jack blushed, and Dansgaard continued. His tone of voice was now harsh.

"We managed to replace one superstition with another. Indeed, if anything, we've dramatically increased the terror in these poor peoples' lives."

"But what choice did we have but to try to save you?" Jack asked.

Dansgaard softened. "Yes, for the moment at least, you have saved our lives. And now I am afraid you'll have to play this hand to the hilt."

"What do you mean?" Julia asked.

"Just look."

The old *galdramaour* had rallied his troops: as he approached cautiously on his mammoth, about half of the community, many of those who had run away, followed, although with considerable fear and reluctance. They stopped about ten meters shy of the Icehawk.

Halldor was obviously nervous, but he summoned up every last bit of dignity and courage to confront the flying boy and girl. Dansgaard translated.

"What are you and why have you come here? What is your monstrous race? Are you human children or *tupilaks*? What is this great bird you have captured?"

Conor immediately responded. "This is my brother, the Wizard of Oz, and his friend, the Good Witch Gilda. I'm the Scarecrow and he—" he pointed to Qav—"is the Tinman. Now, please give us the ruby slippers and we'll click our heels and go back to Kansas."

The kids giggled, while Anaq, who didn't understand Conor's words, smiled bemusedly as he understood that they were making fine fun of Halldor. Even Dansgaard suppressed a grin with difficulty.

"What did the strange one say?" asked Halldor, bewildered.

Dansgaard responded. "He said that the sky boy is his brother and the girl, his cousin. They bring only powers for good."

"Hmmm," replied Halldor, clearly skeptical.

At this point, the kindly woman started shouting at Halldor. One of Halldor's followers, in turn, shouted back at her. Within a few moments one half of the village was screaming at the other half. Some raised their staves. Bjarni tried to calm both sides but no one paid any attention to him.

"Just as I feared," Dansgaard whispered into Jack's ear. "Your appearance has destroyed the unity of the village. Half the people are convinced that you are their new savior, while the other half believes Halldor's claim that you are an evil *tupilak*."

"What can we do?" Jack was beginning to feel guilty.

"We must give them their unity back, by hook or by crook." Dansgaard cleared his throat.

The melee temporarily subsided so that the Vikings could hear him out.

"Kinfolk, please do not fight one another. A divided community, with bitterness in its heart, would not survive two winters in this cold land." Bjarni nodded his agreement.

"There is a simple way to determine who tells the truth and whose magic is more powerful. Let the old *galdramaour* and the young *angekok* duel. That is the custom of both the Norse and the Straelings."

Bjarni now spoke in his archaic Norse. "The old Viking is right. Let not neighbor fight neighbor, but all abide by the result of the magic contest. Halldor, art thou willing?"

Halldor sneered but realized he had little choice but to accept the competition. "Of course. My power derives from my grandfather, the greatest *galdramaour* of all. I will turn this sky boy into a gull and eat his liver for dinner." Some of the crowd laughed.

Qav translated the exchange for Jack, who was incensed by Halldor's arrogance. "Tell the evil stooge that I will turn him into a cow, and the women of the village will milk his udders twice a day!"

This retort drew fervent applause from Jack's fans. Halldor glowered, his face full of fury, and fear.

51. HALLDOR IS DEFEATED

It was agreed that Halldor and Jack would each have a chance to test the other's powers. Jack went first.

"If Halldor's magic is so potent, let him wake my great bird. Indeed, let him fly." Jack pointed to the Icehawk.

Halldor approached cautiously, and those nearest to him could see the beads of sweat forming on his brow. He circled the Icehawk, chanting an ancient Norse incantation.

> *Far niour, fyla*
> *Fjandans limur og gryla;*

> *skal thig joro skyla*
> *en skeytin aursila;*
> *th skalt eymdir yla*
> *og ofan eptir styla,*
> *vesall, snauour vila;*
> *th villiaohilla brila.*[18]

Dansgaard translated:

> *Go down, monster,*
> *devil's scum and witch;*
> *may the earth consume you*
> *and drown you in mud;*
> *you shall howl in pain*
> *and descend into hell,*
> *to lament forever.*

When the incantation didn't work, Halldor tried some howling himself. When his yelling didn't awaken the Icehawk, he nudged the tip of its wing. Then he shrieked some more and threatened the little plane with his magic staff. But still nothing happened. His followers shook their heads and whispered nervously amongst themselves.

Halldor was desperate, so he lifted the wing of the Icehawk and with all his strength shook it. Again, nothing.

Halldor turned to the crowd. "The monster bird is dead. It has no life."

The Vikings look coldly at their disgraced shaman.

Halldor was agitated. "Well, it is my turn to challenge the sky boy. As you know, I have the power to awaken the water oracle—you've all seen me do it. Let this usurper try." Halldor sneered at Jack.

Jack had to think quickly. Most geysers, he recalled, have more or less evenly spaced eruptions. He realized that Halldor had probably figured out the periodicity, and using some method of timekeeping, had fooled the villagers into believing that he controlled its "spirit."

"Qav," he whispered, "ask Bjarni how often the geyser wakes up and when it erupted last."

Qav consulted with Bjarni, who shook his head gravely as he replied. "Bjarni says that it erupts every three days or so, and it last erupted yesterday. Halldor, of course, knows it won't do anything today."

Jack nodded, but he had an idea.

Halldor had folded his arms across his chest. "Come," he taunted, "show us your power."

Jack turned to Julia. "Bring me your magic backpack."

Julia was stunned. "Are you crazy?"

"Do as I say," Jack said in his deepest drama-class voice.

Julia skeptically took her pack off her back and handed it over. Jack reached inside and removed the box of soap powder. He held it over his head.

The kids thought he was mad, but Dansgaard had a sly smile, as if he understood Jack's secret plan.

"Watch real magic work its wonder," Jack said loudly, as Dansgaard translated. He then marched up to the very edge of the geyser's cauldron and poured the entire box of soap powder into its boiling interior. He returned to the base of the geyser.[19]

"Behold!" He pointed to the geyser.

"Have you gone completely daft?" Conor whispered to Jack.

"No, but quick, think of something to chant." Jack felt that his magic needed its own incantation.

With a twinkle in his eye, Conor starting singing, "Hi ho, hi ho, it's off to work we go . . ."

Jack joined in lustily, as did Julia. "Hi ho, hi ho . . ."

The Vikings, awed by the magical song, waited for the geyser to erupt, but after four or five minutes nothing had happened. They began to chatter excitedly to each other. Halldor, initially frozen in fear that Jack's trick might succeed, began to thaw into action.

"See," Halldor declared contemptuously, "the sky boy takes us for fools. He has no power at all."

At that very moment there was a deep rumbling in the throat of the geyser, and a column of superheated water erupted high in the air. The water landed about ten meters from the kids, who immediately moved the Icehawk and themselves out of its scalding range. The eruption continued for a few minutes, then abruptly stopped.

Jack's comrades were almost as stupified by his manipulation of the geyser as the poor Vikings, who flung themselves on the ground in renewed terror and veneration.

Dansgaard whispered into Julia's ear. "The soap powder is an old trick of tour guides in Yellowstone and New Zealand. But what a longshot!"[19]

Jack, somewhat astounded himself, turned to Dansgaard. "It worked!"

"Yes, young man, but you were flying by the seat of your pants. What now?"

Jack, remembering the hungry rumbling in his stomach, turned toward the crowd. "My friends, let us celebrate." Then, scowling at Halldor, he commanded in his best Shakespearan voice: "Be gone, Halldor. Your power is broken."

Halldor, truly crushed, obeyed Jack without protest. He turned his mammoth around and headed off to the north. Most of his former followers, over whom he had reigned so long as a supernatural authority, didn't even bother to watch him depart.

Dansgaard took Jack aside. "Don't get carried away with yourself. You may soon regret having humiliated Halldor so completely. Do you understand?"

Jack accepted the admonishment without protest. Indeed, he was already sorry for overacting, but at least the entire expedition was safe and sound for the time being.

52. THE OTHER SIDE OF VICTORY

Back in the village, Bjarni took charge of preparing a huge feast for the new *galdramaour* and his friends. The Viking people, stunned by the potency of Jack's magic, were again united.

While Jack and Julia snacked on crowberries and sour milk, Dansgaard convened a short expedition meeting.

"Well, my young friends, thank you for saving our old hides. Your courage and resourcefulness have been extraordinary." Anaq nodded his approval as Qav translated.

"But this expedition has turned into a disaster, a calamity for which I take full and complete responsibility." Dansgaard looked truly distressed. The kids were puzzled.

"I don't understand, Professor," began Qav. "Why, we've just opened the most valuable time capsule on earth. This is will be one of the century's most important discoveries . . ."

"Or tragedies," Dansgaard interrupted. "For four of the world's most brilliant budding scientists, you are dunces when it comes to understanding the ethical implications of our foolish blundering. Take the defeat of Halldor, for example."

Now the kids were truly befuddled. "I don't understand," said Julia defensively. "Haven't we liberated these poor people from a curse? Aren't we saving the lives of aging villagers like Bjarni who Halldor would have soon had put to sleep if he remained in power?"

"It is not so simple, Julia." Dansgaard was now truly grave. "Halldor was also the spiritual leader of this community. Despite your allergy to him, I'm convinced he is actually a force for good."

"Professor!" It was Conor this time. "Give us a break. How can you be so softhearted about that hooded ghoul who tried to murder you and Anaq?"

"Once again, Conor, I must remind you that 'murder' was not the concept in Halldor's mind. He genuinely only wished us rest—a sleep, as I have pointed out to you and Qav, that was dictated by the need to control population pressure on these people's scarce resources."

"But now that scarcity is ended," Jack butted in. "There is no need to kidnap new members or gas the old."

"Yes, but that change should have evolved through education and out of the Vikings' own free will. Instead, we have imposed a revolution from above. Now you, Jack, are the new god on their pedestal. And by the way, I fear that we may have turned Halldor toward true evil. Be assured we will hear more from him."

The kids were frustrated by Dansgaard's glum prognostications. They passionately felt they had emancipated the Vikings from a sinister influence, and they didn't really care if Halldor's feelings were hurt. But they respected the Professor too much to challenge his leadership, so Conor changed the subject.

"Professor, what are your ideas about the origin of this community?'

Dansgaard, too, seemed glad to move on to another topic.

"Of course, we still know very little, but from conversations with the villagers, and especially with Halldor during the first day of our captivity, as well as from what we've seen of their culture, it is possible to formulate certain hypotheses."

"We're all ears," said Julia.

"First, like the Pitcairners, these folk are most likely descended from survivors of a single shipwreck, probably a boatload of Greenlanders on their way to Iceland or Norway, say about 1410 or 1420. Some genetic diversity, of course, has been added from time to time by the kidnapping of Greenlanders and perhaps even by a few shipwrecked European whalers."

"How about religion, Professor?" asked Qav. "What happened to Christianity?"

"Indeed, Qav, that is a good question. One would assume that in such fearful isolation, the colonists would have stubbornly clung to their old faith and, in fact, the Norse house was probably their original church. But from the beginning I think there was also another, darker strain of belief in this culture, something that eventually overwhelmed their Christian customs."

"Sorcery?" asked Jack, himself now the chief *galdramaour.*

"Yes. Although most scientists believe that Viking Greenland was driven into extinction by the Norse inability to adapt to climate change—to exchange cattle-raising for seal-hunting, like the Inuit—I've always been skeptical. Certainly the colder, more severe climate of the fifteenth century put great stress on the Norse way of life, but I think the final crisis was essentially supernatural."

"Supernatural?" Qav raised his eyebrows.

"Well, we know that the first witch-burning in Scandinavia occurred in Greenland's West Colony in 1401. During the last decade or two of their existence, the Greenland Vikings were obsessed with witchcraft, spells, and the occult. They made their own nightmares come to life: there was a relentless epidemic of murder in revenge for 'evil eyes'—stillborn babies, dead cattle, and the like. We know this from contemporary reports."

"And these people?" asked Julia, wide-eyed.

"I have a hunch—although nothing more—that the founders of this community were fleeing from the witchcraft catastrophe on the west coast of Greenland. Of course, we have no idea whether they were the accused or the accusers."

"But why would people fleeing from witches themselves end up under the spell of *galdramaours?*" Jack found Dansgaard's explanation inconsistent.

"Because their obsession with witches made them susceptible to rule by witches or wizards. The abandonment of the church suggests that at some point in this lost colony's history, perhaps relatively recently, Christianity was supplanted by the rule of the *galdramaours,* or more accurately, of a crafty *angekok* who took over the role of *galdramaour.*"

"How do you figure that?" said Conor.

"Well, I didn't, initially—it was Anaq who finally helped me solve the puzzle. Qav, ask your grandfather who he thinks Halldor is?"

Qav spoke to Anaq. "He says he's our cousin, the grandson of our missing ancestor, Aua, the last great *angekok* of Tasiilaq." Qav looked shocked.

"Yes, Anaq seems certain of it. And it forms a consistent pattern: a superstitious people in flight from witchcraft, stranded in a bubble in time, their fears magnified by their isolation, were ultimately seduced and dominated by a powerful *angekok*, himself escaping from the Europeans and their alien church."

Julia was trying to think through everything that had been said. "So what you're saying, is that instead of overthrowing the deep structures of these peoples' fear we have simply substituted ourselves in supernatural authority. We've made them fear us more than they feared Halldor."

"Yes, Julia, that's exactly what I think. It would be disastrous for them if we simply packed up and left tomorrow morning—their entire belief system would be in ruins. How would they cope?"

"Well, what options do we have?" asked Qav.

"We must try to find Halldor. We must talk to him," Dansgaard said firmly.

Conor shook his head—everything was becoming confused again.

The villagers prepared a feast that was all the more wonderful for their kindness, although Dansgaard was embarrassed by the unusual attention he received from the young maidens, now celebrating his return from the land of sleep.

Sleep, in fact, was what every member of the expedition now most craved. Despite the Vikings' pleas that Jack take over Halldor's house, he bedded down with Qav and Conor, who had been welcomed back by their original hosts. Anaq and Dansgaard went home with Bjarni, while Julia was whisked away by a friendly young couple and their three children.

Clouds moved in from the sea and it became chillier; by morning it was foggy. Jack, though, felt well-rested, and he happily stuck his dirty face into a bucket of cold water.

"Brrr. Now I really feel awake," he told Qav. Conor was already out, scouting the neighborhood for mammoths.

Suddenly Conor was running toward them at top speed, as if he were being chased by a bear.

"What's scared you? Seen a *tupilak?*" Jack asked jokingly.

"Julia's gone. Halldor kidnapped her last night. He used his sleeping potion on her hosts and then carried her away on the back of his mammoth."

Jack was flushed with anger and anxiety.

"Well, so much for being nice to Halldor," said Qav bitterly.

"Anaq and Dansgaard are at Halldor's complex, waiting for us. Come on, let's go!"

Jack looked up at the darkening sky. "Bad weather for the Icehawk."

"Leave it here for the time being. Let's find out what Dansgaard proposes to do." Conor was insistent.

The two brothers sprinted away, while Qav lingered to give a brief explanation of the events to their horrified hosts. Then he too ran off toward Halldor's, followed by some of the village's young men.

EPISODE NINE: *The Cave of the Dead*

*D*ansgaard was seated at Halldor's table arguing with some of the Viking men, who wanted to track the old sorcerer down and kill him. Indeed, the normally gentle Bjarni suggested that the village would only be safe if Halldor were burnt at the stake.

Jack and Conor burst into the room.

The Vikings lowered their eyes deferentially at the entry of their new *galdamaour.* Then Bjarni's glum face suddenly brightened and he blurted out something that caused Dansgaard to smile. Some of the Vikings chuckled.

"Jack, he says that you should go in your great bird to rescue Julia, then—how should I put it?—let the bird excrete on Halldor's head."

Jack was not amused. "Bad flying weather, Professor. How much danger is Julia in?"

"Calm down a bit—I don't think she is in any immediate danger at all. Halldor kidnapped her because he wants us to follow him. I think he wishes to show us something."

Just then, Qav came in, hugged his grandfather, and sat down next to Jack. "The sky is brewing up something fearful," he warned.

Dansgaard consulted with Bjarni in Icelandic, then with Anaq in Greelandic. "They agree that a blizzard may be on its way, perhaps even one of the dread *piteraqs.*"

Jack reminded Conor that a *piteraq* is a fierce, sometimes hurricane-velocity wind that originates from the pressure differential between the high Inland Ice and the coast.

Bjarni spoke at some length. "He says," translated Dansgaard, "that this is extaordinarily early in the year for such a storm. He fears that Halldor has summoned it in revenge for his defeat, and he reiterates that Halldor must die."

Qav was focused on more practical tasks. "We must leave immediately and try to rescue Julia. But where is Halldor taking her? He has a huge headstart, and if it snows it will become nearly impossible to follow his tracks."

"He has taken her to the Cave of the Dead," explained Dansgaard, "where all of the 'sleepers' rest. According to legend, it is a vast ice cave on the flank of Puisortoq, but none of the locals have ever seen it, because Halldor and his predecessors took the dead there without any escort."

"Conor," Jack asked, "can your infrasound detector help?"

"Well, I don't know if a solitary mammoth would necessarily make signals that it could perceive, but let's give it a try." It took less than ten minutes for Conor to retrieve his equipment from the pile of gear and set it up. He put on the headphones.

"Do you hear anything?" Qav asked anxiously.

"Too much. There's a cacophony, like all the mammoths are talking at the same time. Let me see if I can fine-tune the frequency and range. OK, there's a big conversation very far away, almost at the limit of the equipment's range . . ."

"Could that be Halldor's mammoth?" Jack pressed closer to Conor.

"No, it's a large group in the opposite direction. Must be coming from one of the other valleys. Wait . . . here is another set of signals, very close and approaching . . . it sounds as if it's right outside our door." Conor lifted his head and looked at the professor.

"Don't worry, Conor," reassured Dansgaard, "but can you hear anything else?"

Conor fiddled with the controls, closing his eyes as he strained to hear. "No, I just have the two herd signals, one distant and the other nearby. Wait . . . there is a third signal, very faint and unanswered . . . it must be Halldor's mammoth. Jack, get out your Garmin and let me transfer the coordinates to you."

Jack unholstered the Garmin, and Qav attached a short length of computer cable between the two devices. Almost immediately a flashing cross appeared on the Garmin screen, superimposed on land features that Jack had recorded and saved during his initial overflight.

"*There*, Professor, there . . ." Jack held up the Garmin. Halldor was about twelve miles away, over the rugged mountain ridge that separated the valley from the crevassed nightmare of Puisortoq. The Vikings were speechless at this new display of magic.

Qav had his own Garmin out, studying the location of the signal. "But how are we going to cover that distance in midst of a blizzard?" He repeated his question in Greenlandic to his grandfather.

Anaq smiled and pointed to the door. The three boys went to the portal and looked outside.

The storm was already starting. Hard blown snow stung their eyes, restricting their vision. Then, perhaps a hundred meters away, an astonishing sight: a group of mammoths was being herded in their direction by Viking boys.

The boys closed the door. Conor had an ecstatic expression on his face. "Professor, are we going to use the mammoths? Are we going to cross over to Puisortoq on the backs of mammoths?"

"Yes, Conor, that's the idea. Bjarni claims that only the mammoths can get us through the storm and across the mountains. But I am afraid that not all of you are going."

Conor looked stricken. "Oh, Professor, don't say that . . ." Dansgaard interrupted. "You and Qav are coming with us, but Jack must stay."

Jack looked absolutely crushed, but he didn't say anything.

"Jack, I'm sorry to once again leave you behind. I know that you would risk anything to rescue Julia, but we need you here to man the radio, and if the weather clears, to fly the Icehawk. In a real emergency we'll need you in the air."

Jack looked at the floor. "But how am I to communicate with the locals? What if I need their help launching the Icehawk?"

"Your elementary Greenlandic will probably suffice . . . have you met Ingrid?" Dansgaard pointed to the woman with Inuit features who sat in the corner of the room. She smiled shyly, and Conor and Qav immediately recognized her as the villager who spoke Greenlandic.

"She was rescued by the Vikings as a child when the rest of her family perished off Puisortoq. Her childhood Greenlandic is only marginally better than yours, but the two of you should be able to communicate."

Jack was crestfallen, but he recognized that the professor, as usual, had made the wisest decision. Conor came over and hugged his brother. "Don't worry, Jack, we'll have Julia back by the morning."

Jack was dubious. "But what if this is a trap that Halldor has set? What if he's leading you into some deadly labyrinth?"

Conor winced. Jack was right: Who knew what Halldor *really* had in mind?

56. MAMMOTH COWBOYS

The mammoths, although not as large as Halldor's patriarch, were magnificent. The four females and two bulls were part of the small sub-herd that the Vikings had domesticated for winter travel; like Indian elephants, they had also been trained to assist with heavy chores.

The rescue party consisted of Bjarni, mounted on the largest bull, in the lead, followed by Anaq on the other bull. The two boys, snugly outfitted in double layers of climbing gear and parkas, were mounted on the smallest females, while Dansgaard—magnificent in a polar bear parka borrowed from Halldor's wardrobe—rode the largest female. The final female, bearing tents, food, and extra bear pelts, brought up the rear.

Bjarni explained that it was a rite of passage for Viking boys to learn to ride the great beasts—now it was Conor's and Qav's turn. Unlike the local boys, however, they would have the advantage of mammoth-hair ropes to help them balance.

Although Dansgaard had banned all photography out of respect for the locals, Jack couldn't resist videotaping the hilarious spectacle of Qav attempting to mount his mammoth. While Conor had no problem, the normally poised Qav fell off his mammoth three times in a row. Finally, grimly clinging for dear life to the rope tied around his mammoth's middle, he was ready to ride. The rescuers waved good-bye and rode into the teeth of the blizzard.

Although they were only ten feet apart, Conor and Qav could barely see each other through the snow, much less talk to one another. Instead, sheltering in the deep hoods of their parkas, they used their Garmins to communicate.

"Conor, I can't even see you. This is scary. Are we going to get lost at the outset?"

"Don't worry, the mammoths are used to this. This is why they have evolved infrasonic communication, so they can stay together in storms. But whatever you do, don't lose your Garmin. If you get blown off the back of your mammoth, it's the only way we can find you."

"Roger."

Although the sudden ferocity of the *piteraq*—much like the very worst Irish Sea gale—was disconcerting, Conor felt close to heaven. He was living a fantasy beyond fantasy. His mind, like a berserk computer, was deliriously entering and processing every detail of mammoth behavior. In a half hour he had resolved several of the knottiest problems in megafaunal biology, and who knows what more he could learn before the journey was over?

Dansgaard interrupted his reverie. "Conor," he said over his Garmin, "you're the expert on these infernal devices. Get up front and guide Bjarni—he's losing the trail in the snow."

Conor previously had just been a bump on his mammoth's back, but now he had to take charge and make the beast obey him. Fortunately, as a little boy he had whined, begged, and cajoled his parents at every opportunity to take him to the elephant rides at the Dublin Zoo. (Jack had preferred making faces at the apes.) So, biting his lip, he grabbed the reins in his left hand and slapped the mammoth's ribs with the other.

Like magic, Conor's mammoth shifted into a heavy gait and as he drew the reins to the left, they sped past Anaq and almost ran into the rump of Bjarni's much larger beast. Holding the Garmin in his right hand, he was able to keep Bjarni and the rescue party pointed in the right direction.

Eventually Conor took the lead. He couldn't resist the temptation to call Jack on the Garmin.

"Conor, is that you? Are you alright?"

"Giddy-up" was the only response.

Jack thought to himself, "Oh, god—my brother is now a mammoth cowboy!"

57. FACES IN THE ICE

Julia dreamt that she was trapped in a sticky cobweb, or maybe slowly drowning in a vat of honey. Every time she struggled to awake, she was pulled back down into a heavy, uncomfortable stupor. Finally, she managed to open her eyes.

She was no longer in the Viking house. Although still wearing the same pajamas she'd gone to sleep in, she found herself burrowed inside a warm mound of polar bear fur. In turn, it was enveloped within a delicate fog, a soft white cloud.

With great difficulty she managed to lift herself up on her elbows. Her head immediately started spinning like a crazy top, and she collapsed back onto the bed. She made three other attempts to sit up, but each time she was overcome by grogginess. Finally she succeeded. It took a minute or so for her eyes to adjust to the fog.

She soon realized that she was inside an ice cave. Two seal oil lamps provided eerie, flickering illumination. On each side of her there were designs or impressions of some kind frozen into the blue ice of the walls. As her head began to clear, she stared at the walls with the utmost intensity but still could not quite make out the shapes.

Slowly rising, she wrapped herself in a warm bearskin. "Thank god I sleep in my socks," she thought, as she gingerly tested the very cold and slippery floor. She walked four or five steps toward the wall, then gasped and fell back in horror.

Grotesque faces smiled at her from under a thin layer of ice.

Her immediate instinct was to run, but she held her ground. She closed her eyes for a moment, saying to herself, "Julia, you're a scientist, be brave."

When she opened her eyes again, she could see that the entire wall was a three-dimensional fresco of death. There were scores of upright corpses. Most appeared to be the bodies of elderly people, but there were a few young-looking corpses as well. Their dead faces, for the most part, were frozen in horrible *rictus* grins.

Julia realized that she was in the Viking catacomb, the ice cave where Dansgaard and Anaq had almost ended up. She shuddered at the thought; she had been probably sleeping here for hours. Although she had no recollection of it, she realized that she most likely had been drugged and kidnapped by Halldor.

Once again she had to confront a knot of panic, but she thought to herself: "Fine, now I'm a damsel in distress in a frozen cemetery of dead Vikings. Shall I scream or faint? Or quietly wait to be rescued?"

Fear yielded to anger. For the entire adventure Julia had been, at most, a girl Friday, the sidekick who Jack reluctantly took along on the Icehawk. The boys had made all the rash decisions, undertaken all the heroic feats. She was sick of all this macho posing: it was time for a girl to take charge.

She stuck her tongue out at the laughing cadavers in the wall. "Halldor," she said out loud, "you'd better watch out!" Swaddled inside her polar-bear robe, Julia grabbed a lamp and began to hunt for her abductor.

The mammoths were battling their way up a steep snow slope toward a saddle between serrated peaks. The snow was now so deep that it tickled the bellies of the beasts. The *piteraq* howled like a thousand banshees.

At an earlier stop Bjarni had securely lashed Conor and Qav to their mammoths. Even so, they felt like they were wrestling with the wind for every step of forward progress. Everyone was exhausted by the ordeal, even the stoic mammoths.

Conor, still in the lead, was finally near the summit. The sky was beginning to clear and the snow was subsiding, but the force of the *piteraq* remained undiminished. His mammoth was unable to get any traction and slipped on the icy rock.

Conor had no choice but to dismount. As he untied himself, he immediately was blown off the mammoth's back and fell, sprawling, into the snow. When he tried to stand, the wind knocked him down again—for a second, he thought the *piteraq* might blow him all the way back to Ireland. With difficulty, he managed to lash a knot to the mammoth's waist strap and steady himself. Then, with his head down and his feet dug into the snow for maximum traction, he inched forward.

The final hundred meters of the ascent took the party a half an hour. Conor reached the ridge first. The *piteraq* was now so fierce that his mammoth actually had to sit down for stability. Conor, grasping the reins in one hand and the knotted rope in the other, clung to her side. Eventually he was able to crawl forward to the very edge.

Below him, stretching in three directions to the horizon, was the white hell of Puisortoq, slowly groaning its way to the sea. The great glacier was fractured into a seeming infinity of bottomless chasms and yawning crevasses. It horrified him to think that Julia was trapped somewhere inside that frozen maze.

The rest of the party dismounted. As Dansgaard crawled next to him, Conor showed him the display on the Garmin. The ice cave was somewhere directly below and just slightly to the left. Dansgaard took out a powerful pair of pocket binoculars and scanned the edge of the glacier. He pointed to a gaping hole in the ice far below and handed the binoculars to Conor.

Conor shuddered. The entrance to the cave was, in fact, immense, perhaps five or six stories high and almost half a block wide. There was something uncanny, almost supernatural about it. His delight at being a mammoth cowboy had begun to wear off, and now Conor had to contemplate how much this adventure was beginning to resemble a creepy Edgar Allan Poe story. Next stop: the city of the dead under Puisortoq's treacherous ice.

59. THE SORCERER'S APPRENTICE

Julia's feet were freezing despite her thick woolen socks. Fortuitously, she discovered a cache of Halldor's gear nearby. Rumaging through the strange luggage, she found heavy, fur-lined boots. They were too large, but at least her feet were warm. She imagined that she must now be a terrifying sight.

She resumed her exploration. The dead Vikings were preserved in a section of the cave about 75 meters long containing 150 or 200 frozen cadavers, apparently the total population. That's not surprising, she thought, since ice caves were ephemeral aspects of dynamic glaciers. Cavities like this could probably last for a few centuries at most before being collapsed by the forward creep of the ice.

Julia stopped to look at the first corpse in the hall of death. She assumed he must be the founder of this lineage of frozen souls. He was an extraordinary old man, with the fiercest of dark eyes, and a whispy goatee that resembled Halldor's. Yet Julia was also struck by a certain similarity to Anaq as well.

"Could this Aua?" she asked herself, "the famous sorcerer and Halldor and Anaq's common grandfather? An incredible idea"

Julia, mesmerized by the old man in the ice, didn't notice Halldor approaching from behind until he laid his hand on her shoulder. She jumped but quickly recovered her militant poise.

"So, there you are, Halldor, you miserable charlatan, you fear-monger and kidnapper!"

Halldor, who couldn't understand Julia's fierce words, reacted with meekness, not anger. In his outstretched hand was a bowl of sour milk and berries. He had brought breakfast.

Julia was surprised by Halldor's thoughtfulness. She wolfed down the food and gave the bowl back to him. Disconcertingly, he smiled and then motioned to her to follow him.

Twenty meters further on was a seal oil lamp. Halldor bent down and picked it up.

After about five minutes of walking, Julia could see faint light ahead. Suddenly the tunnel began to open into a bigger chamber which in turn soon yielded to an even larger hall, until finally they were standing in an ice palace that seemed to Julia to be as big as Grand Central Station.

The whole space was suffused with shimmering rainbows. Shafts of sunlight speared the floor through holes in the roof and were refracted by the icy mist. Miniature waterfalls spilled from the sides of the great cavern, and giant icicles grew in its myriad recesses. Julia had never seen anything so sublime, and suddenly she felt a surprising gratitude toward Halldor for bringing her here.

She started forward, but Halldor stopped her. He pointed ahead of their feet. Julia realized that the apparently solid ice was only a thin veneer over a chasm. The entire floor of the cavern was fissured and dangerously crevassed. She shuddered when she realized that she was on the edge of an abyss.

Yet it was all so startlingly beautiful. Down on her hands and knees, with Halldor holding onto her arm, she peered over the edge. Halldor pointed at something with his finger and said "*Tansouk, tansouk!*" Julia's jaw dropped: There, perhaps twenty-five meters below them, was a mammoth petrified in turquoise ice. Its great curved tusks alone penetrated its death shroud of ice.

Halldor then pointed to the left. Much further down in the huge crevasse were the broken figures of two other fallen mammoths.

"I must tell Conor about this," Julia thought. Her mind was aflame with ideas. "Is it possible that mammoths, like African elephants, have graveyards where they go to die in old age? Did Halldor's grandfather follow the mammoths to this cave? Did this suggest the idea of putting the elderly Vikings' bodies in the ice?"

Halldor, seeing that Julia was enraptured, let her stare for a while, then gently tugged on her shoulder. He motioned to her to return to the sanctuary of the funeral chamber.

Julia guessed that Halldor, far from planning to harm her, was actually attempting to teach her. Perhaps she too had become a sorcerer's apprentice.

60. LONDON BRIDGE IS FALLING DOWN!

While Conor and Qav huddled together, shivering behind the windbreak of their resting mammoths, the others debated the next step of the rescue. Dansgaard and Anaq were dubious about the ability of the mammoths to descend the steep mile-long slope to the ice cavern, but Bjarni insisted that the leviathans were more surefooted than most humans.

In the end, the debate was resolved when the great beasts simply voted with their feet. Instantly and in unison, all six of the mammoths pricked up their ears, then gamboled down the hillside without waiting for their riders to remount.

"They hear something. They're responding to infrasound," Conor shouted to Dansgaard, as they hurried behind the animals. In the end Bjarni proved correct, as the mammoths negotiated the slippery gradient with nonchalance, while the humans stumbled, fell, and somersaulted in the treacherous mixture of ice and snow. Even Anaq and Bjarni, the unexcelled hunters, ended up wet and bruised at the bottom.

A seventy-five-meter-high lateral moraine formed the final barrier between the mountain wall and Puisortoq proper. The mammoths immediately found a switchback trail, of sorts, ascending the moraine. In five minutes, the rescuers were on top and looking into the entrance of the great cavern.

There was a smaller cave or ice overhang about 200 meters to the left. There Halldor's mammoth was grazing on a large mound of stored hay. After retrieving their equipment from their pack mammoth, the rescuers let the animals wander off to join their patriarch.

Bjarni, his kind face now free of the painted design that had marked him as condemned to die, was astounded by the wonders that emerged from the packs of the expedition: lengths of climbing rope, ice axes, harnesses, carabiners, and so on.

Dansgaard offered the Viking an energy bar. It would have been a grave violation of etiquette for Bjarni to refuse, and the others couldn't help but laugh as Bjarni slowly chewed the bar with the expression of a man eating a worm—obviously their Viking friend would have preferred a rancid mammoth tail to their organic health food. (In fact, poor Bjarni thought the bar was some kind of animal dropping: strange, the food of these wizards!)

The Professor then gently suggested to Bjarni that he stay behind to guard the mammoths. Bjarni's sigh of relief and his grin suggested that he was not keen to visit the city of the dead.

They divided themselves into two rope teams: Dansgaard with Conor and Anaq with Qav. The boys went first so that if they slipped into a chasm, their bigger partner could sink his axe into the ice and arrest their fall; this was a standard winter mountaineering technique.

But few mountaineers had ever entered an ice cave as big or as dangerously complex as what now confronted them. First, they had to ford an icy stream, then surmount the slippery frozen lip of the cave. Then, amidst a chaos of ice blocks and treacherous crevasses, they had to find whatever route Halldor had used.

"Over here!" Qav and Anaq signaled the other team. A weathered staff, about six feet high and engraved with faint runic inscriptions, marked the true entrance. To their astonishment, they discovered a broad, heavily trod pathway: the trail of dying mammoths.

Within five minutes they entered, from the opposite side, the same wondrous but lethal cathedral of ice that Julia had admired a half hour earlier. Anaq immediately pulled in the rope like a rein around Qav.

"What's wrong, Grandfather?" Anaq pointed to the ground ahead. The solid ice gave way to a thin, precarious glazing over an abyss. In its bowels, Anaq could see the huge cadaver of a mammoth, then another. He gasped.

Conor and Dansgaard were soon at their side. Conor had the same instant reaction as Julia. "Wow! This is just like Africa!"

"What do you mean?" Dansgaard asked.

"In Africa, elderly or sick elephants go to 'graveyards,' usually caves, to die. It's a highly specific behavioral trait of probiscideans."

"How do we get over there?" Qav pointed at a perfectly formed ice tunnel on the other side of the vast pit.

Anaq studied the way ahead with intense scrutiny, then spoke to Dansgaard and Qav, who translated for Conor.

"Grandfather sees two possible routes. We can skirt the abyss by clinging to the wall, but the trail narrows dangerously in the middle." Qav pointed to a tiny ledge that made Conor dizzy even as he looked at it.

"Alternatively, there is that ice bridge in the middle. The ice is much wider, but whether it will support our weight is another question."

"I vote for the ice bridge," said Conor. "The cantilevered section is only five or six meters across. I'm sure it will support us." Conor had done a lot of winter mountaineering in Scotland with his dad and was confident he could tell good ice from bad.

"OK," said Dansgaard with a grin, "you be the leader." Conor gulped and the others laughed.

Tethered by a climbing rope, he approached the ice bridge like a champion diver might his high board. He confidently walked out, his eyes focused straight ahead, but he was secretly humming to himself, "London Bridge is falling down, falling down, falling down . . ."

He stopped in the middle. Although he didn't jump up and down, he shifted his weight back and forth to see if the ice creaked or gave an indication of weakness. It seemed absolutely solid, so he continued to the other side. There was little climbing line left. "Whew!" he thought.

Conor took out some ice screws to anchor the rope, but Dansgaard had already unclipped himself from the safety line.

"What are you doing, Professor?"

"Don't worry, I won't have any problem. But if I did fall, my weight would pull you down with me."

Conor implored him to use the belay, but Dansgaard ignored him and walked across the bridge. As he did, some small pieces of ice and powder fell from the underside.

Qav was next. Belayed securely by Anaq, he had no problem, although again, the bridge shed ice.

Like Dansgaard, Anaq unhooked himself. Qav frowned, and Conor whispered to Dansgaard, "I think the bridge is weakening."

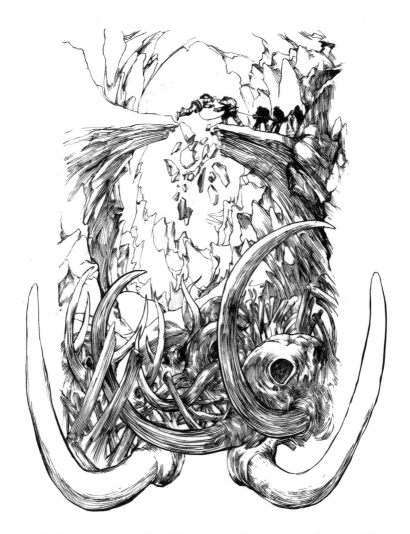

The Professor agreed, and he convinced Anaq to let him establish a belay with the ropes and cleats. Dansgaard clipped himself to the ice screws as well as to both of the solidly sunk ice picks. He then braced his feet for maximum stability. "OK, Anaq, go."

The old hunter shook his head at what he considered to be unnecessary precautions, but he clipped himself back onto the belay line and he confidently started across the bridge. He was slightly more than halfway across when it began to vibrate violently, dropping first large clods, then boulders of ice into the abyss.

"Jump!" Qav screamed.

The old man made a running broad jump that would have brought glory to any high school athlete. His hands reached for Dansgaard as the ice bridge collapsed stories below into the void. Dansgaard pulled his best friend to safety.

The two men chuckled at their close escape.

"Well, I am glad to see that we're not the only two foolish people on this expedition," Qav whispered to Conor.

They were now safe and sound on the other side, but the only route back was the narrow, slippery ledge that gave Conor such jitters.

"Don't worry, we'll cross that bridge when we come to it," said the Professor. Conor rolled his eyes at Dansgaard's bad joke.

61. SLEEPING BEAUTY

Rested for a few minutes, they had the opportunity to admire the wondrous architecture of the great cave.

"This is much bigger than Kverkfjoll." Qav was referring to the famous ice cave in northern Iceland that he and his parents had once visited.[20]

"Yes, but I think it is identical in origin," said Dansgaard.

"Please explain, Professor." Conor was perplexed because most ice caves were scoured by melt water at the front of glaciers, while this cave had been carved in Puisortoq's side, miles from its infamous mouth.

"Hot water from a deep volcanic spring, the same geothermal system that has turned the mammoth valleys into temperate oases, probably extends under part of Puisortoq. That would explain this incredible cave complex as well as the notorious instability of Puisortoq itself.

"OK, let's go get Julia. Don't worry about roping up for now, but put on your lights. The way ahead looks pitch black."

They entered the burial chamber, a perfectly formed ice tunnel about three meters high. Anaq, carrying a powerful flashlight, led the way. Both boys wore divers' lights in headbands.

Almost immediately, Julia saw their faint lights in the distance. Grabbing one of the oil lamps, she ran toward them. Halldor followed reluctantly behind her.

"Jack! Jack!" she yelled, as she almost knocked Anaq over. Qav and Conor ran up to the strange figure in the oversized polar bear suit.

"Julia!"

"Where's Jack?"

Dansgaard interrupted. "I ordered him to stay behind with the Icehawk in case of an emergency. Are you OK?"

Julia was furious with herself for such a stupid display of emotion. She answered calmly, "Yes, Professor, I'm fine. Halldor had no intention of harming me. I think he just wanted us all here. There is something he needs to show us . . ."

Before Julia could finish, there was a loud cry from Anaq, who was now twenty yards further into the catacomb.

Everyone rushed toward him. Anaq was on his knees, with Halldor at his side.

"Grandfather, Grandfather," Qav exclaimed in Greenlandic.

Anaq turned toward him. He wore an expression of reverence and wonderment on his face. "Qav, my child, come meet your great-great-grandfather." Qav kneeled down next to Anaq and Halldor, while the others stood behind them.

They knelt in front of the same patriarch who had previously transfixed Julia, the last great sorcerer of the Ammassalik Inuit and the first *galdramaour* of the gullible Vikings.

After marveling at the man in the ice for some minutes, Halldor looked closely into Anaq's face, then into Qav's. Holding up the oil lamp in one hand, he looked at his own reflection in the ice as he muttered the same phrase again and again. Qav translated it into Greenlandic.

"Kin, Grandfather. He says we are kin."

Anaq grasped Halldor by the shoulders, firmly but affectionately. Then, in the Inuit way, Anaq rubbed his nose on the sorcerer's cheek, while Qav repeated in Icelandic, "Yes, we are your kin, your relatives." Great relief and wonderment passed across Halldor's face, and he hugged both Anaq and Qav in turn.

Conor was deeply touched by this unexpected show of love, as was Julia, who had hoped for just such a moment. Perhaps there was no evil in this place at all, just a misunderstanding amongst peaceful, sometimes frightened people.

Dansgaard, too, was delighted at the family reunion, but he wanted to quickly return with Halldor so that villagers in turn could reconcile with their old *galdramaour.* He said something to Halldor, but instead of answering, the old man grasped both of Dansgaard's hands and looked deeply and sadly into his eyes. Nobody, including the Professor, could quite understand what was happening.

Halldor then gently led Dansgaard further into the catacomb. The others followed a few paces behind. Halldor stopped and peered at the wall, as did Dansgaard, but the Professor, like Julia earlier, initially could not make out the figure in the ice. Halldor raised his lamp so Dansgaard could see more clearly.

Dansgaard emitted a cry that seemed to pierce the very heart of the glacier. It frightened the kids, but Anaq seemed instantly to understand its meaning. Dansgaard, tears flowing into his beard, was clawing at the ice in front of him, as Anaq and Halldor supported him. Then, slowly, Dansgaard regained his composure, his eyes never moving from the ice. He started whispering to the figure in the ice as he rocked back and forth; like someone, thought Julia (who was Jewish) saying the Kaddish for the beloved dead.

Conor and Qav stared at each other, but neither was able to offer the other the slightest explanation of this astonishing behavior. Then Julia whispered, "It must be his young wife, forty years dead."

"Incredible," muttered Qav. "Incredible."

After a while, Dansgaard sat down with his back to the wall, his face drained of its anguish. He seemed almost peaceful now. Addressing no one in particular, he said softly, "Do you see? Halldor never intended any malice. He just wanted to bring us here. So I could sleep with my beloved."

Respectfully, the kids crowded forward to see the figure inside the blue ice. She was a lovely young Greenlandic woman in peaceful repose. Her eyes were closed, and she wore a sweet smile on her lips.

The boys were too awestruck to devote any scientific attention to the young woman's preservation, but Julia scrutinized the body for any signs of trauma indicating her violent death in the sea off Puisortoq. There were none, just as there was no sign of decay.

To Julia this indicated that a very skillful mortician had prepared the body before entombing it in eternal ice. Who put her to sleep?

Halldor's father, or perhaps the young sorcerer himself? Why such devoted attention? Did the young Halldor fall in love with this dead woman? Did he come to the ice cave to visit her? Was it a secret bond he shared with Dansgaard? And, above all, how did he know that she was Dansgaard's wife?

Too bad that Puisortoq had decided that Julia would never learn the answers.

62. AN ICY APOCALYPSE

Dansgaard's reverie might never have been broken had the glacier not begun to move. There was first a soft shower of ice from the ceiling, then a deep bass moan echoed through the tunnel, like a giant sleeper having a nightmare. There was a minute or two of total stillness, then more white powder fell on the expedition's heads.

Everyone looked at Halldor. He was listening intently. When the groaning stopped, he seemed to relax. Suddenly he heard something else. Everyone strained their ears but initially heard nothing, then came a high-pitched sound, like chalk screeching across a blackboard. Halldor instantly jumped up, grabbed Julia by the arm, and barked an order.

"We must get out! Halldor says the cave could collapse!" Qav shouted. He and Conor bolted behind Halldor and Julia. Halfway down the length of the catacomb, they stopped abruptly and looked behind them. Anaq was desperately trying to rouse Dansgaard, who refused to move.

"Wait for a second," Qav yelled at Halldor, then he and Conor ran back to help Anaq. Larger pieces of ice were beginning to fall from the ceiling, and the entire cave was starting to tremble.

"Professor, please, we must go! The cavern may collapse." Dansgaard's eyes seemed to be focused on infinity; he was oblivious to their pleas. Anaq shook him hard, but it had no effect.

Finally Conor pulled on the front of Dansgaard's parka. "Please, Dr. Dansgaard, we'll all die if you don't lead us out of here." It was as if Conor had thrown cold water in Dansgaard's face. He quickly regained his wits.

"Yes, yes, we must leave . . . hurry . . . Anaq and I will follow. Wait for us at the mouth of the catacomb."

Conor and Qav caught up with Julia as Halldor went back to assist Anaq and Dansgaard. A few minutes later, they all stood at the portal of the grand ice palace. The weird keening noise was growing louder, and the ceiling was raining pebble- and fist-sized pieces of ice.

Dansgaard was back in control. He quickly roped Julia to himself and Conor to Qav. "No time for fancy belays, boys. Let Anaq and Halldor lead the way." He offered an ice axe to Anaq, who politely refused it.

The only escape route was along the perilous ledge. Anaq took his boots off and walked in his socks, followed closely by Halldor, perhaps the most surefooted of them all. Conor and Qav were next, then Julia, with the Professor in the rear.

The group inched forward slowly as the unstable glacier began to unleash a death symphony of bizarre and unnerving noises. Suddenly Halldor shouted a warning, and everyone clung as close to the wall as possible. A huge flying buttress of ice the size of an automobile or a mammoth flew by, exploding into a geyser of debris as it hit the true floor of the cave seven or eight stories below.

"Everyone alright?" Dansgaard asked. Anaq was now at the beginning of the nightmare section of the ledge. It was less than half a meter wide, slightly inclined, and very slippery; indentations in the wall offered only minimal handholds for stability.

Anaq said something softly to Qav and began the traverse. Halldor, with surprising grace, followed closely behind his long-lost cousin. Halfway across Anaq started to slip. For a second or two he steadied himself with a firm grip on a knob of ice. Then, horrifyingly, the piece of ice broke off, and he fell.

He plummeted straight down, perhaps two full stories, and crashed onto another ledge with a sickening thud. The ledge shuddered but did not collapse.

Dansgaard shouted down to Anaq. He answered calmly but in obvious pain. "I think I have a broken leg. You can't reach me. Get the kids out of here. As fast as you can. Leave me."

Before Dansgaard could respond, Halldor did something amazing: he started to climb down the wall to rescue his stricken kinsman.

Later the kids would have endless arguments over *exactly* what had happened.

Qav was convinced that it was truly magic: Halldor, like some Inuit-Viking Spiderman, climbed down an impossibly vertical wall. Julia, dispassionate scientist to the core, insisted that it was just a bravura demonstration of ice-climbing skill as Halldor jammed his fingers and feet into tiny crevasses.

Conor wavered in these debates. On the one hand, he admitted that a professional mountaineer could free-climb—if he was so suicidally inclined—such an ice wall. On the other hand, Halldor was an old man, and his feat truly displayed almost supernatural courage and skill.

Halldor quickly reached Anaq's ledge, although he was struck a nasty blow by a baseball-sized fragment of the disintegrating ice ceiling.

Now it was Dansgaard's turn to display agility. Without hesitation he ventured out on the tiny ledge, driving in ice screws, clipping on carabiners, and threading a length of climbing rope. With one hand gripping the rope, he managed to stretch his long legs across the most dangerous section, and straddling the gap, he drove in a final ice screw and secured the rope.

"OK, kids, now you have a handrail. Move quickly."

While Conor and Qav belayed her with the second rope, Julia confidently crossed the ledge. Qav followed, then Conor.

By now the rain of ice debris was becoming deadly. Dansgaard shouted at the kids: "Get out! As fast you can." They obeyed him. The three kids sprinted out of the collapsing cave right into the arms of the worried Bjarni.

Dansgaard meanwhile lowered one of the ropes to Halldor, who doubled it around Anaq's chest. Then Halldor, with a little help from the rope, briskly climbed back to the upper ledge. The professor could see that Halldor's scalp had been badly cut by falling ice.

The two men began to winch Anaq up to them, praying all the while that the ice screws that formed the fulcrum would not pop out of the wall. Anaq helped, as best he could, by using his arms and good leg to reduce weight on the rope.

It was a damnably difficult rescue, and time was running out. Huge cracks were beginning to open in the walls of the cavern, and the groaning of the ice had become a deafening roar.

Finally, Anaq was back to the ledge, one leg grotesquely bent and broken. He was in very great pain. Dansgaard dragged his old friend fifty meters or so, where he met Qav, Conor, and Bjarni. He handed Anaq over to them: "I told you to get out of here! Now do it! Run!"

Dansgaard turned around to see where Halldor was. As the sorcerer ran toward him, the roof started to collapse. It was like a terrible earthquake. Dansgaard was knocked to the floor of the cave opening; although bruised by some large pieces of ice, he was otherwise unhurt. All he could see of Halldor, however, was an arm sticking out of a pile of ice and snow.

Dansgaard dug furiously. He managed to expose Halldor's head, shoulders and arms. Suddenly Bjarni was at his side, and together they pulled the unconscious Halldor free. Behind them an icy apocalypse seemed in progress.

63. A MOMENTOUS DECISION

It was dangerous to linger at the cave mouth, and Dansgaard ordered everyone up the moraine, where Bjarni had already herded the nervous mammoths. It was a hard, at times almost desperate climb, with the waning *piteraq* still lacerating their faces.

At the summit of the moraine there was no time to ponder the sublime sight of the ice cavern's final collapse. Working as a team, Julia and Qav were trying to set Anaq's leg, while Dansgaard and Conor were struggling to revive Halldor. Amazingly, the tough old *galdramaour* had suffered no serious injuries, and within minutes he was sitting up and accepting a drink of water from Bjarni.

Anaq was not so lucky: his femur was severely fractured. Dansgaard was adamant that he had to be evacuated. If they could reach Jack on the Garmin, he could fly the Icehawk high enough to broadcast an SOS to Tasiilaq or Kulusuk.

Anaq, despite his pain, vehemently disagreed. His leg, he explained, could heal perfectly well back in the village—after all, it was not the first time he had broken a bone in the wilderness.

Dansgaard replied that it wasn't just a question of his broken leg. He needed Anaq back in Tasiilaq to establish a lifeline for the Vikings. There was a grave danger that the expedition had inadvertently passed on viruses or bacteria against which the Norse people had no immune resistance. Dansgaard himself would return with Halldor and Bjarni to monitor the health of the villagers and continue his research on mammoth ecology. The outside world could think him killed on Puisortoq.

In the meantime, Anaq, as soon he as he was up and around, could organize a discreet supply trip with vaccines and scientific equipment.

Anaq reluctantly conceded that this made sense. As Qav and Conor suggested that they return in their kayaks, he brusquely cut them off.

"No more Puisortoq."

Dansgaard asked Conor to call Jack on the Garmin while the rest of them set up a tent; Bjarni took the mammoths down the other side fof the moraine where they would be sheltered from the wind as well as less visible from the air by those coming to rescue the expedition.

Conor wasn't sure the Garmin would work with a mountain ridge between them and the village, but he gave it a shot.

"Jack, Jack, can you hear me? Come in."

EPISODE TEN: *The Return*

64. A PLEA FOR HELP

*J*ack had been tinkering with the Icehawk's landing gear, making sure that he could retract the wheels after takeoff so that if necessary he could use the skis for landing on the glacier. Everything seemed in order.

He worried, however, that he might not be able to pick up a signal from the others, so he climbed to the top of the ridge that separated the village from the geyser, and there he waited. The *piteraq*, although subsiding, was still strong enough to force him to shelter behind a large boulder.

Finally, there was a faint communication. "Conor, I can barely hear you. Speak louder."

Conor, who didn't want to alarm Jack with the dramatic details, explained that although Anaq had broken his leg, everyone was safely out of the cave. Then Dansgaard came on the air.

"Jack, we need to evacuate Anaq and the kids, but we can't radio over the horizon. Can you safely get the Icehawk aloft? If you were high enough, your Garmin could probably summon help."

Jack looked around him. The wind still made flying dangerous, but he was anxious to help the professor get a rescue underway—and truly nightmare weather might return if they delayed.

"It's fairly calm here, Professor," Jack fibbed. "I can take off without any problem. The trick will be achieving enough altitude to be able to contact the airport on Kulusuk Island. I may need to climb to four or five thousand feet before the Garmin signal can surmount the horizon."

"Jack, you also need to be evacuated. Can you land here? The top of the moraine is broad and fairly level. But the wind here is still vicious."

"Don't worry, the Icehawk is designed to land on a penny. I can be in the air in ten minutes."

Dansgaard then gave Jack instructions on what to tell the authorities. Jack, in turn, asked the professor to ensure that all the Garmins were broadcasting a directional beacon to guide him, and later, their rescuers.

Jack's departure caused much anxiety in the village. With their old supernatural leader deposed and their new *galdramaour* about to fly off into a vicious *piteraq*, the people were confused and frightened. Some begged Jack not to go, but with Ingrid's help he managed to calm them.

He explained that his father, the Sun, had ordered him to fly to heaven and scold the god of storms for unleashing the unseasonal *piteraq*. He told them not to worry: the expedition would return shortly and life would be better than ever in the Valley of the Runes.

As he took off, the Vikings were awestruck at the ease with which the young sorcerer was able to rouse his giant bird from its sleep. Some were frightened when the creature began its fierce leap into the sky. Jack circled twice over his constituents, waving and dipping his wings in reassurance as the villagers cheered.

At ground level the dissipated *piteraq* manifested itself as simply a strong tailwind, but as Jack fought for altitude the air currents became more powerful and chaotic. "The old god of storms," he thought to himself, "is trying to slap my little plane out of the sky like a giant might swat an obnoxious fly." He was glad Julia was safe on the ground.

Although he had attained sufficient altitude to cross the ridge toward Puisortoq, he needed to go much higher to surmount the over-the-horizon radio problem. But every hundred feet gained was at the expense of an increasingly brutal battering—he was David fighting an invisible Goliath. The Icehawk was hurled down, then pitched back up, shaken from side to side, and almost turned upside down. Jack received an unexpected cram lesson in dangerous, seat-of-the-pants flying.

Finally he was almost in the layer of stratus clouds, about a mile high according to his altimeter. "Kulusuk, come in, come in. Mayday, Mayday, please come in." He used the expedition's emergency code name, drawn from the initials of its two elder leaders. "This is Able Dog. Can you hear me?"

The air was so turbulent that Jack feared that the very wings of the Icehawk might be ripped off, but he persisted on the Garmin. "Kulusuk, Mayday. This is Able Dog. We have an emergency."

Suddenly there was a response, first in Danish, then in English.

"Able Dog, we hear you. What is your status?"

"Dansgaard lost his life in a crevasse. Anaq has a broken leg and cannot walk. The rest of us are OK."

"Give us your position."

Jack relayed the directional beacon from the expedition's Garmins to the rescue center on Kulusuk Island. The radio operator was horrified.

"My god, you're on Puisortoq! Where are we supposed to land?"

Jack tried to calm the official. "No, we're on the glacier's southern lateral moraine. There's a good landing surface. We'll put out flares."

Kulusuk base was still incredulous that the expedition was on Puisortoq, but they reassured Jack that they could reach them within a few hours. "You are lucky this freak storm is almost over and that the big chopper is here."

The Air Greenland Sikorsky 61—the only helicopter with the capability to rescue the expedition—was usually based at Scoresbysund, seven hundred miles north of Tasiilaq. Fortuitously it had been flown to Kulusuk earlier in the week for some routine maintenance.

"Thanks. We'll await your arrival. Able Dog over and out." Just then there was a terrible vibration in the trike, but it wasn't caused by the wind. Jack looked up. One of the structural braces in the left wing had cracked. The entire wing might break in half any moment.

Jack had to land immediately. Circling over the high mountain ridge that separated the Valley of the Runes from Puisortoq, he carefully banked his wounded little plane into a spiral of descent. With his right foot he pushed down his landing wheels until they locked into place. He kept looking nervously at the injured wing, which was beginning to flex and lose its aerodynamic geometry. The Icehawk was becoming increasingly difficult to control.

4,500. 4,300. 4,000. 3,800 feet . . . He spiraled east of the expedition's camp, banked, then came down the axis of the lateral moraine on the south flank of Puisortoq. Far in the distance he could see red tents, then a flare.

He felt a violent jerk as the last foot or so of the wing tip snapped off. Jack was almost flipped upside down, and he frantically struggled for control. 1,800. 1,500. 1,200 feet . . . the ground was coming toward him at terrifying velocity. He pulled desperately on the control bar.

He was able to slow the descent and keep the trike within a rough glide path, but the wings were oscillating wildly and he was afraid he would land on his side. He had an image of the Icehawk catapulting end over end. It was not a pretty picture.

66. MAGICAL LANDING

Julia was the first to see the Icehawk high in the sky to the west. Its motion was no longer the smooth path of a raptor, but rather the erratic zigzag of a giant bug. She realized that it was being badly buffeted by the wind.

Jack was in trouble.

She called out to the rest of the expedition, and they came running. Qav ignited their sole flare.

Conor instantly recognized that something was wrong with the Icehawk. He could see that it was rolling from side to side, on the brink of a catastrophic somersault. If his brother lost control of the trike now, he wouldn't have the faintest chance of survival.

Halldor at first had difficulty understanding what was happening, but as the Icehawk careened closer, he knew that the great bird was trying to kill Jack. He removed his cloak and climbed up on top of the boulder. With his hand raised above his head, he started a violent incantation.

While Julia and Conor were too petrified to pay any attention to Halldor's jumping and shouting, Qav thought it a stupid, foolish gesture.

Jack was headed straight for them, but with one wing canted sharply to the side. If the wing hit the moraine first, it would flip the Icehawk over and destroy it.

Conor, who had tears in his eyes, muttered, "Please, Jack, please, pull your wing up." It looked hopeless.

Then Halldor gave a mighty shout—simultaneously, Jack regained control and righted the wing. The kids looked at the old *galdramaour* in amazement.

Jack touched down gracefully, although as he bumped along the surface of the moraine a rock broke one of his tiny landing wheels and the Icehawk spun completely around in a circle.

As he unbuckled his harness, he said, "I thought I was a goner. I was coming in on my side, then suddenly I was able to pull my wing up and land on my wheels. It was like magic."

Indeed. Very old-fashioned magic.

67. MAMMOTH GOOD-BYES

There was no time to waste. The old Vikings, who now included Dansgaard as well as Halldor and Bjarni, had to return immediately to the village with the mammoths. They had to be across the pass and out of sight by the time the rescue helicopter arrived from Kulusuk. There was no opportunity for extended farewells.

Dansgaard began by apologizing to the kids for first having exposed them to so many dangers and now forcing them to lie to the authorities about the circumstances of his disappearance. Julia cut him off.

"Professor, it is no deceit to do our duty to protect the Vikings and the mammoths from the potentially disastrous intervention of the outside world. But we'll miss you greatly, even as we continue to stay in touch through Anaq." She kissed Dansgaard on the cheek, and the old scientist blushed. The boys hugged him.

Dansgaard looked at all of them through moistened eyes and said: "Don't worry, I'll be in your dreams." Jack knew exactly what he meant.

There were also hugs for Bjarni, their gentle friend who would now help lead the Vikings in their gradual transition toward contact with modernity.

For Halldor, who they once had despised as a cruel tyrant, there was an extraordinary reconciliation. After Conor and Qav described how he had stood magnificently on the top of the boulder, hurling his magic at the angry sky in a desperate attempt to save Jack, the young *galdramaour* decided it was time to restore dignity to his elder.

With Dansgaard translating, Jack handed his Garmin to Halldor. "Here, Halldor, is my magic talking rock. You are truly the greatest of *galdramaours* and I am but your student." He embarrassed Halldor with a hug, as did the other kids. The old sorcerer had tears in his eyes.

There was one final leave-taking. Conor climbed down to the other side of the moraine to say good bye to his mammoth. He petted its extended trunk, and the giant probsicidean replied with a baritone purr.

68. LEFT BEHIND

The huge Sikorsky helicopter hovered over the heads of the children. They talked to the crew with their Garmins. The pilot told Qav that they were going to lower a medical team first before attempting to land.

Two figures in orange flightsuits gracefully slid down the ropes from the open bay door of the copter. One was a co-pilot, who immediately ran ahead to mark out a safe landing zone; the other was Qav's dad, East Greenland's famed flying doctor.

Qav hugged his father, then took him to the tent where Anaq was lying. They emerged a few minutes later. Qav's father was deeply upset and angry.

"Your grandfather will be fine, but this is the last time he'll ever be allowed to gamble anyone's life in these reckless adventures." The kids started to explain but then realized that there was no point in arguing.

The big helicopter landed, and the crew quickly ushered the kids aboard. Anaq was placed on a stretcher, and his son persuaded him to accept an injection of powerful painkillers. The old hunter quickly fell into a deep sleep.

On the flight back to Tasiilaq, almost no one spoke. The kids huddled close to each other: Julia held Jack's hand; Jack had his arm around Conor, whose shoulder, in turn, was a pillow for Qav. They had become a tight-knit family.

But after four days of the most astounding adventure and discovery, they were also in a state of shock. They were heartbroken to be leaving their secret Ice Age world and its gentle people. They dreaded the inevitable interrogations they would have to endure by the officials and their own families. And although they knew they were doing the right thing, they still felt like juvenile delinquents.

Jack was also troubled by a guilty sense of having left something or someone behind. It wasn't the Icehawk, now a small relic on the moraine:

he would build a new, more powerful version, incorporating everything that he had learned from his dramatic flight tests. Something else was bothering him.

"Julia!"

She jumped. "What, Jack?"

"Anori."

"Oh, no." They had left behind at Tingmiuriut the great golden dog, and it might be weeks before the fishing boat was recovered. Would Anori starve or be lost?

69. A SURPRISING REUNION

The helicopter landed outside Tasiilaq. An ambulance stood waiting to take Anaq, still unconscious, straight to the regional hospital. Also waiting on the ground was most of the local population. Qav hadn't seen so many people at the helipad since the last visit by Greenland's Home Rule prime minister two years before.

Anaq was removed first, then the kids climbed out. The crowd cheered.

Qav looked at Conor. Both felt guilty about the stories they now had to tell. Dansgaard's irresponsible leadership, his tragic "death," and the harrowing rescue of Anaq and the kids had become headline news throughout the world. There was grave concern about how the science summer school had gone so dangerously astray, and the United Nations was planning to investigate.

While Dansgaard had become the "posthumous" object of much criticism, the kids themselves were treated as great heroes. They found this extremely embarrassing, and so they kept to themselves, using every opportunity to sneak off away.

Julia, Jack, and Conor had only one more day left in Tasiilaq. Their moms, as well as Jack and Conor's older sister Roisin, were arriving to take them home, respectively, to New York and Dublin. Qav, meanwhile, was being sent back to Copenhagen, indefinitely, to keep him away from his grandfather.

"We're going to be broken up and grounded," Conor complained.

"All the more reason for us to keep this expedition together, forever if need be. We have email—and we can talk every day. We'll figure out a way to reorganize." Julia was absolutely defiant.

In the meantime, the kids had an urgent errand: before anyone arrived from the Danish Polar Institute to take over Dansgaard's lab, they had to spirit away the mammoth bones, notes, and photographs. The newcomers must find no evidence of the mammoths. They agreed to revisit the lab at midnight.

There was an extraordinary surprise waiting for them. As if he had never left, Anori, the Viking elkhound, was guarding the lab door.

"Where did you come from?" The kids were both astonished and greatly relieved.

The giant dog looked absolutely well fed and healthy. Indeed, there was almost a twinkle in his eye. Had Anori brought an enigmatic message from Dansgaard? Another mystery was added to the heap.

It was agreed that Julia and Conor would split up the mammoth research, taking notes and specimens back to their respective homes. They had invented a "Reindeer Ecology" project as a cover for their continuing research on the mammoths.

70. "NUKA"

A second set of farewells occurred the next day at the helicopter pad. Anaq was still in the hospital, but he had smuggled out a message via Qav. "Grandfather says, simply, 'stay brave'." In return, what could the kids say to the extraordinary hunter who had taught them so much?

Julia and Jack were already onboard the shuttle helicopter, discussing the surprising coincidence that both of them were applying to the same university: Caltech in Southern California. Conor lingered at the door. It was damned difficult business saying goodbye to your best friend.

"Guess what?"

"Yeah, Qav?"

"I have a discovered the Inuit word for 'mad Irishman'."

"What's that?"

"*Nuka.*" Qav squeezed Conor's arm, then turned and ran away.

Conor, moist-eyed, buckled himself into his seat. "Jack, can I ask you a question?"

"Shoot."

"What does *nuka* mean in Greenlandic?"

"It means 'much-loved brother'." He put Conor in a playful headlock as Julia laughed.

N O T E S (for big kids and science buffs)

1. H. Ostermann, ed. "Knud Rasmussen's Posthumous Notes on the Life and Doings of the East Greenlanders in Olden Times," *Meddelelser Om Gronland* 109:1 (Copenhagen, 1938). (Puisortoq).

2. The last native reindeer/caribou were seen in the Scoresbysund area of East Greenland in 1899. (A small herd was later reintroduced to Ammassalik Island.) Meanwhile, the white polar wolf, once common in East Greenland, became locally extinct due to overhunting in the 1920s. See the discussion in Ejnar Mikkelsen's great saga of Arctic survival and unbreakable friendship, *Two Against the Ice* (South Royalton, Vt.: Steerforth Press, 2003), p. 14. (Originally published in Danish, 1955). See also "Vanished Men and Beasts," in Helge Ingstad, *East of the Great Glacier* (New York: Knopf, 1937).

3. Inspired by Edgar Allan Poe's *The Narrative of Arthur Gordon Pym;* Verne's 1864 *A Journey to the Center of the Earth* included runic messages and living mastodons.

4. The Cape York meteorites had been the exclusive basis of an Arctic Iron Age dating back fifteen hundred years or more to the predecessors of the modern Greenland Inuit, the so-called Dorset people. See Robert McGhee, *Ancient People of the Arctic* (Vancouver, B.C.: University of British Columbia Press, 1996), pp. 201–02.

5. Col. Bernt Balchen, et al., *War Below Zero: The Battle for Greenland* (Boston: Houghton Mifflin, 1944); and David Howarth, *The Sledge Patrol* (London: Collins, 1957).

6. The dwarf mammoths on Southern California's Channel Islands (*Mammuthus exilis*) were half the size of their Imperial mammoth ancestors, while the pygmy proboscideans of Sicily and Malta (*Palaeoloxodon falconeri*) were only one-quarter of their forebears' stature. See Larry Agenbroad, *Pygmy (Dwarf) Mammoths of the Channel Islands of California* (Hot Springs, S.D.: Mammoth Site of Hot Springs, 1998).

7. For an exciting account of contemporary efforts to bring *Mammuthus* back to life, see Richard Stone, *Mammoth: The Resurrection of an Ice Age Giant* (New York: Basic Books, 2001).

8. "It is more reasonable to believe that the East Greenlanders are a mixture of Old Norse and Eskimos." Holm quoted in Vilhajlmur Stefansson, *Greenland* (London: Harrap, 1943), p. 249.

9. Qav is teaching Conor the technique used by Maligiaq, the Greenland national kayak champion. Video clips can be viewed at www.qajaqusa.org, the authoritative website for Greenland-style kayaking.

10. Stefansson, *Greenland*, pp. 70–72 (Irish in Greenland).

11. Gary Haynes, *Mammoths, Mastodonts, and Elephants: Biology, Behavior, and the Fossil Record* (Cambridge: Cambridge University Press, 1991), pp. 57–58 (infrasound communication).

12. Paul-Emile Victor, *The Great Hunger* (London: Hutchinson, 1955) (East Greenland famine).

13. Lawrence Millman, *Last Places: A Journey in the North* (Boston: Houghton Mifflin, 1990), p. 198.

14. "Although oppressed and dwarfed, wooly mammoth could exist on Wrangel Island until at least 3,700 years ago. . . . The extraordinary fact is not that mammoth eventually became extinct on Wrangel like elsewhere, but that, together with some relics of tundra-steppe flora, it was able to survive the early Holocene environmental revolution in this Arctic island refuge." Russian scientists quoted in Claudine Cohen, *The Fate of the Mammoth: Fossils, Myth, and History*, trans. William Rodarmor (Chicago: University of Chicago Press, 2002), pp. 244–45.

15. Millman, *Last Places*, p. 199.

16. Kirsten Hastrup, *Nature and Policy in Iceland, 1400–1800: An Anthropological Analysis of History and Mentality* (Oxford: Clarendon Press; New York: Oxford University Press, 1990), pp. 212–228.

17. For a fascinating account of the 20,000-year-old "mammoth-bone orchestra" found at Mezin in the Ukraine, see Adrian Lister and Paul Bahn, *Mammoths* (New York: Macmillan, 1994), p. 108.

18. This is a song from the *Snaefajallavisur*, "the most forceful magic poetry in Iceland," used to exorcise devils and expel spirits. See Hastrup, *Nature and Policy in Iceland, 1400–1800*, p. 219.

19. Soap disrupts the surface tension in the geyser's calderon. One of the most famous examples is Lady Knox Geyser in New Zealand: in the late 1800s a group of prison laborers attempted to wash their garments in what they thought was a hot spring, but the laundry soap caused a huge eruption that scattered their clothes over acres. Since 1933 the geyser has been soaped daily to assure timely eruptions for tourist crowds.

20. Kverkfjoll, on the northern rim of the Vatnajokull glacier, was first explored by a French expedition in the 1980s. The earth's largest known ice caves and abysses are in the Greenland Icecap (the Inland Ice) itself; some may be almost a kilometer deep.

MIKE DAVIS is the father of Roisin, Jack, James and Cassandra. A MacArthur Fellow, he is the author of *City of Quartz, Ecology of Fear, Magical Urbanism, Dead Cities,* and other books. He lives in San Diego.

XOXOX

WILLIAM SIMPSON belongs to Christopher, Conor, Wendy, three dogs, a cat, and a mouse! He has idled away his past seventeen years, in Northern Ireland, producing artwork for diverse comic strips, books and feature films . . . with the occasional exhibition thrown in for good measure.